SEDUCTION

Love in London, Book 2

LAUREN SMITH

OTHER TITLES BY LAUREN SMITH

Historical
The League of Rogues Series
Wicked Designs
His Wicked Seduction
Her Wicked Proposal
Wicked Rivals
Her Wicked Longing
His Wicked Embrace
The Earl of Pembroke
His Wicked Secret
The Last Wicked Rogue
The Seduction Series
The Duelist's Seduction
The Rakehell's Seduction
The Rogue's Seduction
The Gentleman's Seduction
Standalone Stories
Tempted by A Rogue
Sins and Scandals
An Earl By Any Other Name

A Gentleman Never Surrenders
A Scottish Lord for Christmas

Contemporary
The Surrender Series
The Gilded Cuff
The Gilded Cage
The Gilded Chain
The Darkest Hour
Love In London
Forbidden
Seduction
Climax
Forever Be Mine

Paranormal
Dark Seductions Series
The Shadows of Stormclyffe Hall
The Love Bites Series
The Bite of Winter
Brothers of Ash and Fire
Grigori
Mikhail
Rurik

Sci-Fi Romance
Cyborg Genesis Series
Across the Stars

For Angela, Jeanne, Amanda, and Amy, who work tirelessly to help make each story shine!

❧ I ❧

Bloody Hell.

Tristan Kingsley was in a dark spiral. Anger and confusion raged beneath his skin like wildfire. His mother had sent his carefully constructed plan toppling down like a house of cards when she'd announced her engagement to an American investment banker.

Her engagement wasn't the *worst* part of the whole situation. No, the fucking demons in hell were laughing at him for the ironic twist his destiny had just taken. Because five minutes ago, Katherine Roberts had walked through the door with her father, Clayton.

My Kat. The girl he'd ruthlessly pursued and sweetly seduced until she'd succumbed and let him take her to bed. The girl he'd fucked so hard she'd had trouble walking the next morning. The girl he'd opened up to about things he'd never shared with anyone. And he still hadn't had enough of her to satisfy his obsession.

My stepsister. Future stepsister. And, two nights ago, they'd rammed his headboard into the wall so hard, it had left gouges in the wallpaper. He'd had rough, wild sex before, but with her... She'd been so innocent, a bloody virgin, but she'd responded like a sex goddess...

I can't think about her anymore. How her body felt underneath me—skin to skin. How perfect she tasted. How she screamed out my name when I exploded inside of her...

Kat hadn't moved from the doorway to the library of his mother's townhouse. The moment she'd come in the door and recognized him she'd frozen. Her face pale, her lips pursed, and her gray eyes wide as saucers. She hadn't known this was coming, just as he hadn't.

It was a bloody nightmare.

They'd left Cambridge separately for their Christmas holidays, each facing the same situation. His mother had told him that she was in a relationship with someone, and Kat's father had told her the same. Neither he nor Kat could have guessed that their parents had met in London and started dating. Or gotten engaged. It was a strange, and now damnable, coincidence. Of all the eligible men in London his mother could have met and fallen in love with, it had to be Kat's father?

At twenty-five years old and working toward his Master's in business, Tristan could afford little time for distractions, aside from the string of nameless girls he'd slept with before Kat. He had classes and the pressures of his father's estate looming over him. That was the price he had to pay for being the future Earl of Pembroke.

Until he'd walked into the Pickerel Inn pub one night and his world had changed forever. Kat, a luscious, intoxicating first-year undergraduate, had walked up to the bar for a drink and they'd talked. Something had seemed to pull them together, like invisible strings. She'd leaned up on her tiptoes and kissed him. The way she'd felt in his arms, her lips melding with his... In an instant he'd gone from a man who could have any woman he wanted to a man who wanted *only* her. She was nineteen, and so inexperienced, he wanted to drag her back to his bed and never let her leave until he'd shown her everything he knew about the art of sexual pleasure.

My obsession, my erotic fantasy. Mine. All mine.

At least she had been until his mum had blown his plans to hell with the news that Kat was going to be his stepsister. As a stepsister, a family relation, she'd be untouchable. Their parents simply wouldn't allow it. He'd had plenty of encounters with protective fathers in the past when stories of women he'd seduced had come out in the papers. But Tristan had always held his ground, had never done the honorable thing and married any of those girls. It was just sex. This wasn't the Victorian era. If a woman went to bed with him, that was her choice and no father could demand Tristan that do anything afterward.

I've never been a saint. I certainly can't be one now, not when I want Kat as badly as I do. But how was he going to get Kat all to himself if his mother and her father were watching over them both during the holidays? He'd have to find a way to keep their relationship a secret. It was the only solution. And if the paparazzi ever got wind of his affair with Kat, his father would have him executed in the square of the London Tower just to make a point.

Kat was completely unsuitable—at least she would be in his father's eyes. And for the moment, his father still had a firm grip on Tristan's future, including whom he could date. As an American with no titles, no connections, and no vast fortune, she offered nothing that his father would approve of. Tristan clenched his jaw. He despised that his father had so much control over his life, but that was how it had always been. As the only heir to the estate, he had a duty to the land and the people who worked on it to keep things afloat. His father still controlled the family purse strings, and Tristan knew he couldn't abandon the estate.

Knowing his father would never approve of Kat didn't stop Tristan from wanting her, and it certainly didn't deter him from his intent to sleep with her again. It simply made him all the more aware that he'd have to be careful about how he got her back into his bed so that no parents could discover them.

His mother, Elizabeth, was still standing by Kat, and she made a tiny gesture with her head, encouraging him to come over to his future stepsister. All he wanted to do was walk over and kiss Kat senseless…but their parents were staring at him.

I ought to get out of here before I make an arse of myself.

How was he going to survive three weeks with Kat under the same roof and not touch her whenever he wanted?

"Tristan, don't be rude. Stop sulking by the fireplace, come over here and say hello," his mother hissed in admonishment.

He walked over to Kat and held out a hand, pretending they'd never met, never touched, *never* shared his bed, exploring each other's bodies. It was harder than he expected to resist reacting to her. He smiled politely, fighting off the urge to chuckle when her pale cheeks blossomed with color.

She must be remembering, as he was, how it had felt when he'd pinned her down and made her beg for him to do a thousand dirty, erotic things to her. And he had, oh, he had. And that was making it so hard to keep from reacting with the intimacy he desired. There wouldn't be a scorching kiss, no stroking of hands. Not while their parents watched them with hawk-like precision.

"It's lovely to meet you, Kat." He sucked in a breath as she slowly took his hand and shook it. Sparks of heat burst between their palms, that undeniable chemistry that drew him like a planet orbiting a star. Cosmic, inescapable. This was why he couldn't walk away, why he had to touch her, keep her close to him. She was the first woman that had fascinated him both in bed and out.

She seemed to be trapped in a daze, their hands still connected. Her gray eyes were full of desire, but he could see she was trying to suppress it.

"Hi," she said finally.

He could tell by her ashen face that she was only going to get out the one word and nothing else. Her full lips quivered, and he longed to haul her into his arms and kiss her, perhaps bite those lips playfully until she smiled again.

Why wasn't she like every other girl he'd slept with? They'd been forgotten the moment they'd left his bed. A parade of pretty faces and nothing more. But he knew every freckle on Kat's face, every curve of her tempting body, how her mouth felt as she'd explored his skin, eager, and yet new to the experience of sex. How could he ever forget being with her? There was no way he'd give her up, not when there was so much left to discover between them.

They were both damned now.

"I'll show Katherine to a guest room. You and Clayton can plan the evening while I see her settled," Tristan offered, needing, *hoping* for one minute alone with her.

"Excellent idea, Tristan." His mother's beaming face made his body flood with a dark tide of guilt.

All he wanted was to talk to her. They needed a plan. Neither of their parents could ever find out they'd slept together. They had to keep everything secret.

"Follow me, Kat." He almost reached for her hand, but caught himself just inches from her wrist. Pulling back his arm, he forced himself to keep his distance.

"Thank you, Tristan." Kat's father smiled, too, curling an arm around Lizzy's waist.

Tristan swallowed hard and nodded, but didn't linger. He

didn't want to endure public displays of affection involving his mother. *Too bloody awkward.*

Kat followed him out of the drawing room, closing the door behind her. The second the door was shut he grabbed her hand, wild inside with the need to touch her. He knew they shouldn't continue this...whatever it was between them, but right now, as he held her hand, none of that mattered.

To hell with our parents. I want her.

"Tristan," she whispered, her breath catching as he pulled her down the hall to the stairs that led to the upper floors.

"This way."

"Where are we going?" she asked as they climbed the steps.

"Somewhere we can talk," he muttered and tugged her into the nearest guest bedroom.

The instant they were alone inside the room, he shoved her against the closed door and gave in to his desire. Kissing her hard, he unleashed an explosion of lust and need that had made him hard the moment he'd seen her in the drawing room. He delved into her mouth, seeking her tongue, and she met him boldly, her lips just as eager. He caught her wrists and jerked them above her head, pinning them with one hand.

It felt so bloody good to kiss her again. How sweet she tasted, how soft and feminine she felt against his body. God, he'd missed this, and he'd only been without her a few days. Using his other hand, he stroked down her side, cupped her round arse, making her hips buck against his touch.

It had only been two days since they'd parted from his room in Cambridge. Two bloody days that had felt like an eternity without Kat in his arms. He'd wanted to see her before he left for London, but he'd had to leave right away. Fuck, he needed to take her here, right now, against the door.

Panting, he rocked against her, relishing the little sounds

of pleasure she made when he used his body to cage hers while they kissed. Each time his lips touched hers, he fell deeper into a trance of pleasure that silenced the world outside their shared breaths. There was never enough; he would always crave her with this wild madness. The American knew just what to do with her pink little tongue to make his cock ache...

I'm going to lose my fucking mind.

Their mouths finally parted, and Tristan rested his forehead against hers, his eyes closed as he relished the control he had over her and the closeness of their bodies. It would be so easy to ravish her right here; she wanted it, too. The little minx was staring up at him with those silver-gray eyes, like polished moonstones gleaming with lust. The shivers racking her body made him all the more hungry to take her right there, but it was too much of a risk with their parents so close. Lord, he hated how clear that one thought was. Their parents were downstairs talking about wedding plans, and he was up here, ready to take his future stepsister to bed. Talk about scandalous. Sure, they weren't blood related, but most people would turn a disapproving eye on this situation.

When he opened his eyes, he saw tears on Kat's cheeks.

Tears?

Confusion jolted though him like an electric shock. He dropped his hand from her wrists, and she lowered her arms, wrapping them around herself.

"Kat, darling, what's the matter?" He lifted a hand to touch her cheek, but she shied away and darted around him. When she put the bed between them, something hard knotted in his stomach. "Kat?"

"Tristan, how long have you known?" she demanded.

"Known what?"

"About our parents. How long have you known they were dating?" Silent accusations glittered in her eyes.

Kat thought he'd kept that from her? His heart kicked against his ribs. He wouldn't lie to her, she *had* to know that. Tristan was many things, but a liar wasn't one of them.

"I *didn't* know, I swear to you. Not until you walked in the door, and Mother said your name. I only knew my mother's new fiancé had a daughter. She never mentioned a name. Kat, the odds of this happening..." He gestured around them. "That our parents would get together?" He began to pace, unable to stand still with all the pent-up energy crackling inside him. "Honestly, Kat, I didn't know." He paused, facing her.

Those damnable tears still covered her cheeks. There was nothing worse than watching a woman cry. He couldn't stop it, couldn't undo whatever had hurt her. Moving toward her again, he reached out to cup her shoulders. Kat dodged his grasp.

"Why won't you let me touch you?" That look of hurt in her eyes was killing him, and he couldn't explain why. He needed to hold her.

"Tristan, our parents are *engaged*. Don't you get it? We can't be together. If my dad ever found us like this, he'd freak out. This has to stop."

Stop? He couldn't let her go. There was no chance of that.

"No, I—"

"I mean it, Tristan. I won't jeopardize my father's happiness. Not for good sex."

"Great sex," he corrected.

Her little smile in response was melancholy. "Great sex. It's not going to happen again. Do you understand?" Her cheeks flushed, and her chin lifted in a show of strength. It was one of the things he loved about her, how strong she was, but he didn't want her strong now, not when she was resisting what lay between them.

"I can handle your father, Kat," he promised. "They would

never have to know we're together." If Kat wanted to be with him, he would find a way to keep it a secret from their parents.

She drew in a fortifying breath and pulled her hair back from her face as she exhaled.

"It will only end badly. No matter what happens. They can never know about us, and we can't *ever* do what we did again. We're going to be brother and sister. Even if it's just stepsiblings, that's still...not okay. People will talk, and I don't want that. Tell me you understand, and that you agree we have to stay away from each other."

No. Every instinct inside him was shouting to deny her request. What they'd shared couldn't be abandoned and couldn't be thrown away just because it was forbidden.

"Kat, I want *you*. What happened between us, that doesn't happen every day." He took a step toward her, but she held up a hand.

Those tears shimmered like diamonds on her skin. Beautiful and shattering at the same time.

"Please, just go. I need some time alone."

Alone? How was she going to be alone at a time like this? They were all trapped in the same house for three weeks. He didn't want to leave her so she could cry by herself. He knew that was what she was going to do; the pain of her decision to end things between them was all over her face. Just like the last time, when she'd told him to get out of her dorm room.

Tristan weighed the options of trying to kiss her again, or at least hold her, but it didn't seem likely he'd succeed. She'd raised her chin, and her kissable lips were set in a firm line. It would be better if he waited. Gave her time to breathe. Once she'd had time to cool off, he'd be able to reason with her. He didn't like the idea of patience, but he sensed that if he pressed her now he might lose her. And he couldn't lose her, not again.

"Very well," he said, backing away. But it was a long moment before he was able to compose himself. He paused after opening the door. "Please don't push me away, Kat."

She didn't look at him. That hit him like a punch to the gut. Stepping outside, he closed her door and leaned back against it. Tristan tilted his head back, staring at the ceiling.

"Tristan." A masculine voice jerked him from his thoughts.

Kat's father was standing there, hands in his pockets, watching him, his gaze penetrating. He was a man, Tristan thought, who would easily figure out if his daughter was being seduced by his future stepson.

If Tristan wanted to get Kat beneath him on a bed he'd have to be very stealthy.

"Mr. Roberts." He nodded in greeting.

"Is my daughter all right?" Clayton asked, his brows knitted together. He walked up to Tristan, and Tristan had a distinct impression the other man was measuring him up, while trying not to make his observations too overt. Just as Tristan was doing.

"She's a bit overwhelmed, I believe." Not a lie exactly.

Clayton Roberts cleared his throat and shuffled his shoes on the carpet. "Ahh, I knew this would be a shock to her and I should've waited for all of this, given her more time, but..." He paused and raised his head. "I love your mother very much and didn't *want* to wait."

The man was open and honest, and Tristan couldn't hate him for that. His mother had lived a hellish existence while married to his father. She deserved a good man, one who would love her the way his father had failed to.

"Then you'd better take good care of her." It wasn't a threat, but he'd be happy to make it one if Clayton didn't.

The American simply laughed. Did they always act so odd about such serious things? Kat certainly did.

"I will," Clayton promised. "It's not every day a man is given a second chance at happiness."

"Good." Tristan didn't really know what to say. He felt awkward talking to this stranger who would become his stepfather. He was used to being in a position of power around other men, but this wasn't a situation he could have prepared for.

Fucking hell. When Carter found out about this... His best friend would laugh clear through next week.

"I'll check on Kat," Clayton said, offering a warm but hesitant smile. "Why don't you let your mother know we'll be down for dinner later?"

"I will," Tristan replied. With a sinking feeling deep in his chest he walked away from Kat's door.

❦   2   ❦

Kat sat on her bed, knees tucked up to her chest, arms curled around her shins. Tears dripped down her cheeks, soaking her jeans in two little damp patches on her knees. Everything inside her was a jumbled mess of pain and confusion, all of it so thick and strangling she could barely breathe.

Dad's engaged, and my future stepbrother is Tristan Kingsley. My Tristan.

Two weeks ago I saw him walk into a pub and kissed him because I wanted to experience an adventure. Two days ago I gave him my virginity, and we shared the most mind-blowing sex ever. Now he's here...and he's going to be part of my family.

I'm so screwed.

It didn't change how she felt about him. He was gorgeous, not just on the outside, but inside, too. Their first night together, he'd confessed things, small whispers in the dark about himself. What filled him with joy, made his heart beat fast. Things a man wouldn't share unless he really wanted to. He'd opened up to her, and she'd done the same in return.

That has to mean something doesn't it?

He was sexy, addictive, so electric in bed that he'd left her more spellbound with every kiss, every caress. Everyone said having sex for the first time would be painful, awkward, and unsatisfying. Not with Tristan. He'd fulfilled every fantasy she'd ever had. The dark brooding bad boy, one who dominated her senses with his mouth, his exploring hands, his power over her, yet never making her feel she couldn't tell him no if she wasn't ready. They'd made love all night in his bed at the grand Fox Hill estate while the snow fell outside the windows. All she had needed was him. Nothing else had mattered.

Kat closed her eyes, still feeling his hands around her wrists, the way he'd pinned her against the door. It made her body flush with heat and her blood pound in her ears. How did he know just what to do to make her unravel from the inside out? Why couldn't she go back to Cambridge and his bed where it was just the two of them? She needed him to touch her, to make her feel alive, to show her that exquisite world of pleasure he'd only given her a taste of two days ago.

But now I can't have him. He's going to be my stepbrother.

It didn't get any more off-limits than that. Her dad would freak out if he ever found out she and Tristan had... She shook her head. Clayton had always been protective, and he'd never approve of her dating someone older than she was. And Tristan was twenty-five to her nineteen. A six-year difference.

God, this was so bad, so bad. She didn't want to think about how she'd have to spend not just this Christmas but all holidays to come around him and survive not being with him. Because if she was being totally honest with herself...it wasn't just her dad finding out that scared her. It was how easy it would be to fall in love with Tristan. The more time they spent together, the harder it became to go their separate ways. Love was dangerous. Love burned a person up inside.

She'd watched it destroy her father's life after her mother had left.

I don't ever want that to happen to me.

The thought of that agonizing pain, that awful crushing of one's heart...it was something she never wanted to experience. But Tristan had the power to do that to her. She'd gotten her heart involved when she opened herself up to him and shared parts of herself she'd never shared with anyone else. And he'd shared himself right back. Still, she feared he wouldn't feel the same way about her. A man like Tristan didn't fall in love; he had too many woman out there to seduce, and she was just his current obsession, God only knew why.

Sniffling, she wiped her hands across her cheeks, trying to get rid of her tears. Maybe her dad getting married to Lizzy was a good thing. Tristan being off-limits as a stepbrother would make it easier for her to stay away from him. It would protect her heart. She'd had her adventure, she'd slept with him and almost fallen in love. It was as close as she could allow herself to get without risking her heart.

I just have to find a way to steer clear of him for three weeks. No matter how hard it is, I have to resist him.

Kat closed her eyes, memories of him flooding her until she couldn't ignore them.

Every time she'd see his hands, she'd remember how he had pressed her down on the mattress as he hovered over her body. She had to watch his mouth as he spoke and not think of the sinful way those lips had sucked on the tips of her breasts, or how he'd licked her in secret places that had made her scream his name until she was hoarse. He had shown her that pleasure wasn't just physical. Every time they'd been close, not just in bed, she'd felt alive, as though every part of her body and soul reached out to his, connecting them. His laughter had filled her heart, and his flirty smile had stolen her breath. And she couldn't forget the way he had looked at her when they first met, as if there'd been no one else in the room...

The guestroom door opened, and her father's head appeared around the edge. She jerked, her face flaming. *Thank God he couldn't hear her thoughts.*

"Hey, honey, mind if I come in for a minute?"

Her day couldn't get any worse. "Sure." She shifted to sit cross-legged as her dad closed the door and walked over to sit on the bed.

He ran his hand through his dark hair and sighed. There was a weariness in his eyes that hadn't been there moments before.

I've done that to him. I wasn't happy about this whole engagement thing.

Sure she could fake some smiles and politeness, but her father knew her better than that. Guilt gnawed at her insides, and she fought the sting of fresh tears in her eyes. It was selfish to want him all to herself and to have Tristan all to herself, too. And she hated herself for that.

Her father eased down on the bed beside her, his large hand touching hers, familiar and comforting.

"Come here, honey," he murmured.

She moved closer, and he wrapped an arm around her shoulders, making her lean over so he could press a kiss to her forehead and hug her tightly. In that moment, hurting the way she was, she felt as if she were twelve years old. She was supposed to be mature for her age, not prone to crying or acting out. She wanted to be an adult in her father's eyes, not a child needing protection. More important, she wanted to be a woman whom someone like Tristan would admire and respect. Even though they couldn't be together, she still wanted him to like her.

"I screwed up. I realize that. I should have told you about

Lizzy much sooner." He rubbed her arm in the rough-but-gentle way only fathers seemed to manage.

Kat sat there, numb inside, as she listened to his deep, rumbling voice. For so long it had been just the two of them. Her mother had bailed on them once she'd realized how hard parenthood would be, and Kat's father had spent the last ten years proving that they hadn't needed her. That the two of them could do just fine on their own.

Everything was going to change now. And Tristan as her new stepbrother? It was so messed up she couldn't even think about it without a throbbing pulse beating right behind her eyes.

"Kat, please talk to me," her father begged. "It's okay if you're upset or angry, but don't shut me out." He gave her shoulder a little pat.

Where would I even begin? "Hey, Dad, I'm so glad you just up and decided to marry some woman without talking to me. Oh, and by the way, I totally slept with my future stepbrother, but that's cool, right? Yeah, her dad might have a heart attack.

"I know it's a lot to take in," Clayton said.

"You just dumped this on me, and I can't be instantly happy for you." The comment slipped out, crueler than she meant it.

"I'm sorry, Kat. I wish you could understand. The last several years have been...lonely for me. When your mother left, I gave up being happy." He turned his face away, his chin dropping silently. "I was convinced I'd never love again, *could* never love again. She was my first love, Kat. It's not easy to get over losing that."

An image of Tristan, smiling, holding her in bed flashed across her mind.

She crushed that thought, grinding it to dust. That was lust. Pure and simple. *Not love.*

"When you fall in love for the first time everything is new

and exciting, sometimes scary. It's all fire and love and passion. If that fire goes out, the cold that follows... It scars you, soul deep."

Kat stared at her father, her own heart splintering inside her chest as she watched him bare his soul to her. They'd never talked about her mother. *Never.*

"I'm sorry, Dad," she whispered and leaned into him, resting her head on his shoulder. He put his arm around her again.

"It's not your fault. It took me ten years to learn that it wasn't *us* she left. It was the concept of a family that troubled her. It meant she had to be a part of our team. And that's what families are. A team." He finally looked down at her again and smiled. "I want you to be open to adding Lizzy and Tristan to our team, our family. I know you don't know them yet, but I think you'll like them."

Kat winced. She couldn't confess just how well she did know Tristan.

She rubbed her palms on her jeans before looking at him. "How did you know you loved her?"

"Your mother?"

With a little shake of her head, she dropped her gaze again. "Lizzy. How did you know?"

Clayton grinned, and the expression lit up his entire face. When had he ever looked so happy? Not in a *long* time. The man had put the *work* in workaholic. He claimed he never had time for dating, yet Lizzy had changed that *and* him. Kat wanted to know what had pushed her father to act so out of character. She needed to understand why he'd want to take a risk with his heart again after what had happened when her mother had left.

"She makes me smile. When we first met, she *saw* me, just me. Not my money, not my job. It's so easy to talk to her, she listens, and I love to listen back. It's something I never had with your mother. An openness of the heart we were both missing in our first marriages. Neither of us expected or planned this, but it happened, and I can't imagine life without her now." Her father tilted her chin back and studied her face. "Someday you'll fall in love, and it will change you forever."

Kat thought of monarch butterflies and the way the caterpillars formed chrysalises and then, after a period of time, were reborn. They could never go back to being caterpillars. Falling in love was a type of metamorphosis. But it was a dangerous one, for her heart.

"She makes you happy?" Kat asked, even though she knew the answer.

"Yes, very happy."

Kat ducked her head. So Lizzy was here to stay because she made Dad happy. That meant Tristan wasn't going anywhere anytime soon and he was definitely going to be her stepbrother. How in the hell was she going to survive the holidays?

"Now, will you join us for our first family dinner in a couple of hours, after you settle in?"

"Yes." She could do that. Dinner would be easy. All she had to do was eat, right? Then why did the very thought of it make her stomach turn?

"Good." Her father rose from her bed and kissed her forehead again. "I'll see you in a bit."

"Uh-huh." She waited until he'd gone before she threw herself back upon the bed and stared up at the four-poster bed hangings over her head.

She had to admit, Lizzy had excellent taste in interior design. The town house was beautiful. Just like Fox Hill, Lizzy's house in Cambridge. Everything the woman touched was perfect. Just like Tristan. He had that same golden touch his mother had when it came to beautiful things and beautiful houses. Like his bedroom at Fox Hill. And his bed... That thought led to other thoughts of them in that bed, bodies entwined, sharing moans and breathless whispers.

Oh no, I can't go there.

I just need to survive dinner and lie low. If I avoid Tristan, he'll give up and leave me alone. I'll be able to forget about our mind-blowing perfect night together, and we won't break up our parents' marriage. And I won't let him carve his name in my heart.

That invisible pressure of his hands on her body was there again, haunting her, lingering in her mind and her senses. She shivered. "Damn it."

⚜ 3 ⚜

"Tristan." His mother's call halted him in his tracks on the way to his bedroom.

"Hello, Mum," he said as he spotted her at the end of the hall near the doorway to the small upstairs study.

"Might I have a quick word?" She rubbed her palms together nervously.

Shoving his hands into his pockets, he walked over to her and followed her into the study.

She closed the door behind them and faced him. "I know we haven't talked much tonight, but now we have a chance." She waited, biting her lip and smoothing her hands over her white cashmere sweater.

"I'm happy to talk, Mum." He would humor her, but he wasn't going to start this conversation.

"Well, what do you think of them? Kat seems like a lovely girl. Clayton says she's shy, but a wonderful student. Did you know she's attending Cambridge, just like you? She's only a freshman, but maybe you will have a chance to see her when you both return after holiday."

He almost smiled. Tristan planned on doing just that,

seeing lots of Kat *in his bed*. Preferably with her ankles thrown over his shoulders and her sweet cries of ecstasy filling his ears as she begged him to fuck her harder. He cleared his throat and attempted to put that delicious thought on hold.

"They seem very nice, Mum. I hope you've thought this through, though. Father won't be pleased..." He walked over to one of the couches and stretched out on it.

"Let me worry about your father. And yes, I *have* thought this through. I want you to like Clayton and Kat." Lizzy took a chair opposite him. "It's important to me that you do. We're going to be a family, Tristan. He and I want to spend the rest of our lives together."

Tristan folded his arms over his abdomen and met his mother's concerned gaze. "Does he make you happy?"

A warm, unguarded smile touched her lips. "He does. And he makes me laugh. I didn't know love could be like that. With your father..." A red blush stained her cheeks, and she turned her face toward the window. Weak winter light penetrated the thick panes of glass and illuminated her hair, bringing out the hints of red amid the darker brown.

"You don't need to talk about him, Mum." He drummed his fingers on his stomach.

"I know." She laughed softly, a mixture of chagrin and amusement in her tone that made him smile. It had been too long since he'd heard her sound so content. If Kat's dad made his mother laugh, that was a good thing.

With a sigh of resignation, she faced him. "We do need to talk about your father, though. He's demanded that you be at the estate for Christmas. We both know how he gets when you don't do what he wants."

Her words drew forth a quarter-century of dark memories. Cold holidays, icy dinners, frosty exchanges over afternoon tea. Never a kind word, never a single utterance of praise or affection. And always that knowledge that his father's word was law. Whatever the old boy wished, it had to be done, or else someone would pay dearly for defying his orders.

The Earl of Pembroke was an absolutely wretched human being and an even worse husband and father. It was no surprise that the local papers in London loved to drag out any negative news about him when they could. Usually they used Tristan to do it, smearing the papers with photos of affairs and lovers, trying to tie him to his father and his father's political agenda in the House of Lords.

"You'll talk to him, won't you?" his mother asked. "Smooth things over for Christmas?"

"I'll call him tomorrow. He won't get more than a few days from me, though."

His mother's smile wilted at the corners. "Be careful, Tristan." She cleared her throat and then changed the subject. "How's Carter doing?"

Tristan shrugged. "Carter is well. Still in love with Celia."

"He is such a delightful young man. If only her parents weren't so opposed to him."

Indeed. Parental opposition was the death of many relationships in a society like his. The peerage of Britain had standards, and they forced them to be met, albeit quite secretly. A relationship with Kat, for example, would be permitted as a temporary dalliance, but never a marriage.

Not that he intended to marry Kat—she was only nineteen and far too young to marry anyone—but when he did marry, his father was going to attempt to pick his bride as though they were stuck in the Victorian Age. Therefore, he had every intention of delaying marriage to anyone as along as possible. He wanted to enjoy his bachelor years while he could, which included being with Kat. He was going to have Kat in his bed again, and he wouldn't let something like his father's disapproval slice through what lay between them. If they had to build a world of secrets to keep their relationship hidden, he would do whatever was necessary to have her. He'd give her some time, some space...but he would get her back in his bed, right where she belonged.

Just when I thought life didn't challenge me anymore... He chuckled.

"What's amused you, sweetheart?" His mother raised one elegant brow. As a boy, that tone and questioning gaze had made him confess many sins. Now he was made of sterner stuff.

"I was merely thinking of Carter and Celia." He rarely lied to his mother, but this was necessary.

If she ever learned of his interest in Kat, his mother could upset all his plans. She would swoop in and carry Kat away to safety, far out of his reach. She'd never been blind to his activities. Along with most of London, she'd seen him in the papers and knew his levels of debauchery.

"You know," his mother paused, "you should give Kat a tour of the house tonight." His mother rose from her chair, resting one hand on the top of the wingback. "I want her to feel comfortable here. After we get married, they'll be moving in, since Clayton's flat is too tiny for all of us. Besides"—his mother sighed wistfully—"I love this house. It's a relief Clayton doesn't mind my choosing my place over his."

Tristan wondered how Kat would feel about moving in here during the school holidays. He remembered that night in Kat's dorm room when she'd explained why she loved books so much and how she'd never had a place to settle down for long. They were friends she could take with her, she'd said, friends she'd never had to say good-bye to. She'd confessed this in the dim, warm confines of her little bed that first night, when they'd slept together without sex. Even though he'd wanted to bed her more than anything, he'd bided his time, enjoyed feeling her in his arms, controlling their first foray into the land of pleasure without actually getting inside her body the way he'd wanted most.

He'd wound his arms around her, and something deep in his chest had twisted painfully as he listened to her open her heart. It hadn't lessened the raging lust to possess this girl, but it had softened that animal hunger, deepened it... He'd held her closer, tighter, wanting to ease his ache and her own. Unable to resist getting close to her, he'd shared with her his love of maps, and the way stained glass filled him with strong, powerful emotions.

Yes, there was much he and Kat had yet to learn about each other, but he would make sure they would have the time.

He'd never wanted to be with just one woman before, but he was starting to see the appeal of having a relationship of some kind with her. The more he learned about Kat, the more she learned about him, the more intense their bed play was. He craved the way bedding her made him feel. Powerful, exhilarated, uninhibited, and completely free, yet bound to her at the same time.

I need to be careful. My taking Kat to bed could ruin my mother's happiness.

Tristan sat up on the couch and studied his mother. When his father had left the pair of them alone for weeks at a time while he'd seen to his duties on the estate or handled matters in Parliament, she'd brought Tristan to Fox Hill. After he'd grown up, she'd started spending more time in London at the town house she'd acquired after the divorce. It offered her a way to stay in the middle of town and not feel so isolated while she rebuilt her life.

He'd grown to love this house and Fox Hill as much as she did. For his mother to suggest that someone besides him would live here was her way of opening up and showing the world she was ready to live, now that love was back in her life. Tristan couldn't help but admire her.

"Promise me you'll be nice to Kat. Clayton says she doesn't have many friends because they've moved so often. Neither of them are used to this way of living either, with cooks, servants, and drivers. As her older brother—"

"*Stepbrother*," he cut in. That distinction was vitally important, given what he planned to do to her in his bed.

"Er...yes," his mother nodded. "Stepbrother. She would benefit from having someone like you to show her London and introduce her to people. It would be perfect during the holidays to take her to see all the sights."

"I think that is a lovely idea, Mum." He grinned so broadly that his cheeks hurt as he leaned back into the couch and crossed his hands behind his head.

Take Kat about London? His mother had unwittingly provided him the perfect way to slowly entice Kat back into his bed. He'd have to pretend he had no intention of seducing her, though. He would play the polite, friendly stepbrother she wanted him to be. For now.

You will be mine again, sweet Kat.

❦

Kat had just stepped out of the shower and wrapped a towel around her body when she heard the doorknob rattle.

"Just a minute!" It was probably her dad trying to check on her.

The brass knob rattled again.

"Almost done," she said as she tucked the towel more firmly about her body, mentally smacking herself for forgetting to pack her long robe.

When she unlocked the door, it flew open instantly. A shirtless Tristan stood there, holding a towel, looking down at her with those hypnotic blue-green eyes.

Her eyes, without approval from her brain, swept down

over his body: the sculpted abs, the indentations of his pelvic muscles, and the way his jeans hung low on his hips. Hips she'd held and dug her nails into the other night as he'd pounded into her. Her lower body twisted and clenched with sudden desire at the mere memory of his raw, powerful possession of her. She couldn't forget the feel of his body, pressing her down, his cock filling her until she couldn't breathe. The way he'd *owned* every part of her.

Damn. How had she convinced herself that avoiding him was a good idea? Right now she wanted to drop the towel and beg him to take her, damn the consequences.

"Are you finished?" His tone was pleasant. No hint of fire, no branding scorch of his gaze…just politeness. He was doing exactly what she'd asked him to do. Treat her like a stepsister he'd only just met. Before today's awful revelation of their parents' engagement, he would have smirked at her, teased, and tried to steal the towel… A pang of longing for the playful part of him swept through her. God, she missed that.

What would it take to win one little smile from him, one that was meant for her, and not tempered by his polite distance.

I asked for this. It didn't make her feel any better.

"I'm done." Heat rushed to her face from embarrassment at her inner thoughts. Thankfully he had *no idea* how conflicted she was feeling right now. Or how her body was reacting to being so close to him and being denied his touch. Like a thirsty woman crawling across a Saharan desert and glimpsing an island oasis only to discover it was a mirage.

He made a low, gruff noise, not exactly a response, but it sent shivers through her. She couldn't forget the sounds he'd made in bed two nights ago. He'd been half-animal, growling, nipping, showing her a rough side to passion, one she knew she would always crave. Tristan had pierced a dark part of her sexual side, exposing it to the light, and she couldn't deny that it existed, nor did she *want* to.

He slid past her, their bodies brushed in the narrow space of the doorway. Heat exploded through her, and she froze, trying to control her reaction to him.

Tristan froze, too, their bodies pressed close. His warm breath fanned her cheeks and his natural masculine scent enveloped her. Memories of their night together came flooding back, no matter how she tried to keep it out.

He lifted his hand to her cheek, pausing a second before he would have touched her. She met his gaze, her breaths shallow as his lips twitched in a ghost of a smile. Then he brushed his knuckles over her skin. Fire rippled in the wake of that "barely there" caress. Every part of her was aware of him and his closeness.

Would it be so hard to keep a relationship between them a secret from their parents? Maybe they could...

"Please..." she begged, unsure of what she really wanted.

"Please, what?" he replied, in that dark, low tone that made her purr inside like a cat in heat. He slowly backed her into the wall next to the shower, closing the door behind him. He placed his hands on either side of her head, caging her in, and lowered his face to hers.

A feather-light, teasing kiss. A nip at her bottom lip. She clenched her thighs together, feeling the rush of wet heat in response to his subtle aggression. How could he affect her like this? His touch, his kiss, sent her body into riotous waves of longing for him.

He nuzzled her neck, licking and nibbling on the sensitive spots that sent electric pulses from her head to her toes.

Kat grabbed his shoulders, digging her fingers into his hot, bare skin. The towel around her body stretched against her breasts as she struggled to control her breathing.

His hands dropped from the wall to her waist, tugging on the folds of the towel that barely covered her.

It would be so easy, he could lift my towel up and fuck me right here against the wall. Just one more time, we could...

The towel dropped to the floor.

Tristan's eyes raked over her naked body, and when he lifted his head and met her gaze, one corner of his mouth slid into a lazy half-grin that hit her so hard her knees knocked together.

He lifted one finger, pressed it to his lips, and made a soft "Shhh" before he leaned down to kiss her collarbone. Her nipples pebbled with the cool air and her building arousal. She stared down at the top of Tristan's head, noting the way the light brought out hints of copper in the dark locks. His kisses traveled down in a slow, teasing path to one of her breasts. When he flicked his tongue against one sensitive peak, a whimper escaped her.

He is going to kill me. Right here in the bathroom of his mother's house... *Holy fuck*...

Her hands moved to grip his hair, but he caught her wrists and pinned them against the wall by her hips.

"Oh, God," she panted as he knelt in front of her and glanced up, that wicked grin curving his lips upward. There was no denying the magnetic pull of that smile and how it obliterated all of her defenses.

Tristan lifted one of her legs up, putting her calf over his shoulder, opening her to him. Kat dug her nails into the wall, praying she could keep her balance. Tristan's lips danced lightly down from her navel to her mound. His lips settled around her clit, which pulsed hard and sharp. The tip of his tongue stroked, flicked, and played with the swollen bud. As he teased her with his mouth, his hand coasted up her inner thigh before it found her wet entrance. Drawing lazy, slow patterns in her tender flesh, Tristan tortured her with exquisite agony. Kat squirmed, writhed, pleaded in little soft desperate sounds for him to stop, to keep going...to...

"Ahh!" Kat gasped as he licked at her.

The pulsating sense of need, was too great to deny. The explosive climax hit her hard, and she threw her head back, swallowing her cry of pleasure when his hands dug into her ass, holding her in place while he drew out her orgasm, lapping at her folds until she was too sensitive to do anything but beg for mercy. Currents of desire rippled through her, not diminished at all by the fact that she'd just come apart with his mouth on her.

The wicked glint in Tristan's eyes was her only warning that he had no intention of stopping. He started to dip his head toward her mound again with a throaty chuckle.

"*Please*..." she rasped frantically, dying to have him take her. It didn't matter what happened outside the door, they were here together and he was going to...

"Kat?" Her father knocked on the bathroom door.

She sucked in a breath, and Tristan's hands, which were stroking her outer thighs, stilled, his muscles tensing beneath her palms. Neither of them moved. Neither of them dared to breathe. Her heart pounded so hard that she couldn't hear anything outside of that thunderous racing beat in her ears.

"Kat, are you okay?" her father asked, rapping his knuckles on the door again.

Tristan rose silently to his feet to tower over her again. His blue-green eyes cut through her as he stared down at her. "Answer him, before he opens the door." It was barely a whisper but she was close enough to hear him.

She cleared her throat, her mouth dry. "I'm fine, Dad. Be out in a few minutes." She closed her eyes, praying her dad wouldn't break the first rule of the father-daughter code and come inside without her express permission.

"Okay, honey."

Her ears strained to pick up on the sounds of his departure. When several seconds had passed, she sagged against the wall, letting go of Tristan's arms. Then she dove for the bath towel and flung it around her body.

"We can't do this again." She met his gaze, surprised at the flicker of anger in his eyes.

His sensual, full lips thinned into a hard line, and his eyes narrowed, the fire in them dimming. His jaw clenched, and he turned his face away as though he didn't want to look at her. He was mad, and she couldn't blame him. They'd lost control right here in the bathroom because the magnetic pull between them was too strong. Sexual frustration coursed through her, and she bit her lip, focusing on the sting of pain to get her mind off of how much she wished she had surrendered to him completely and how he'd have been deep inside her right now if she had.

He moved away to pull a towel from a rack above the toilet and dropped it on the counter. Then he glanced over his shoulder.

"Mum has asked me to give you a tour of the house so you'll know where everything is while you're here. I'll meet you outside your room in half an hour." Then he turned to face the shower.

As he leaned into the stall and flicked the faucet handle to turn the water on, Kat watched the muscles of his back play in little ripples. The faintest trace of claw marks still cut across his shoulder blades. *Her* marks. Again, that flood of primal desire and animal satisfaction moved through her. She wanted to make more, to permanently claim this gorgeous man as hers.

But he's not mine, not anymore. I can't have him because it will put our parents, and my heart, at risk. That last part was her deepest fear. She'd started to care about him, to get addicted to him, not just physically but emotionally. She didn't want to get her heart broken. She'd grown up watching her father live with a shattered heart and she didn't want that to happen to her. What if she wasn't strong enough to survive that level of heartache?

The sound of his pants zipper had her jolting back to awareness and hastily ducking out of the bathroom. The last thing she needed was to catch a glimpse of him in anything less than jeans. After how he'd just gone down on her, she was having a hard time convincing herself she shouldn't want to return the favor... Her libido and self-control couldn't handle that. Flushing guiltily, she clutched her towel around her body and dashed back to her room. How was she going to get through this? With Tristan sleeping just down the hall, naked, the way he'd told her he did...

Shit, I'm in too deep here. I want him too much... How am I going to survive three weeks with him being so close?

¥ 4 ¥

I *can survive this. As long as I don't think about his perfect abs, or his tight ass, or his lips... Yeah, no more thinking about Mr. Sexy-as-Hell.*

Kat threw on a pair of jeans and a warm cable-knit sweater and stared at herself in the mirror. They were eating at home, so she hoped jeans would be okay. What if there were more than three courses? What if there were half a dozen different spoons on the table? How would she know which ones to use?

There really ought to be a list of basic rules or a manual or something. *Ten ways to please your British Bad Boy in bed and impress his mother at dinner...*

Kat leaned toward her reflection in the full-length mirror, feeling completely stupid as she put on mascara and lip gloss. It was okay to want to look nice, right? That was what she wanted. It had *nothing* to do with Tristan. *Definitely* not. There was nothing wrong with wanting to look nice, except... she'd never really cared about it before tonight. Before Tristan. Kat let out a little hiss of frustration and stalked over to her bed. She grabbed her backpack and dug through its contents until she found what she was looking for.

Dropped from the Clouds.

When she'd packed for this trip to London, knowing she'd meet her father's girlfriend and son, she'd reached for this book first, relishing the way it felt like a security blanket. Normally she would have brought her well-loved paperback, but she'd wanted a part of Tristan with her when meeting Lizzy for the first time. So she'd carefully wrapped his gift in a vellum cloth and tucked it in a safe place in her bag, where it wouldn't be damaged.

She remembered Tristan's face when he'd watched her pull it out of the box that night. Eager anticipation and joy had illuminated his face in a way that had made him glow. He'd really given thought as to what to buy her. It hadn't been anything generic or clichéd. No, the man had to go and be perfect by buying her a book that had meaning to her and proving he'd listened to her.

Touching its gilded cover and tracing the balloon on its surface made her think of Tristan. As foolish as it had been, she thought she'd be carrying a piece of him with her, like a shield into battle. But now he was on the other side.

She plopped down on the bed and tried to read a few pages, but her mind kept drifting toward that encounter with Tristan in the bathroom. What if she'd let him seduce her right there, take her against the wall of the bathroom, with their parents so close? The forbidden track of her thoughts made her shiver. His large hands had played with the folds of her towel, teasing, as though he'd planned to tug it from her body.

The man loved to get her naked. She remembered how he'd stripped her out of her clothes at Fox Hill, peeling her dress off her body with a deliberately slow pace, heightening her hunger to be taken by him. The arousal then, just as in the bathroom today, had built to a point where she hadn't been able to think...only to feel what he did to her. Being with him was like a drug—it robbed her of all control

She wasn't aware of how much time had passed before someone knocked on the door. Glancing at her watch, she flinched. She'd been staring at the wall for the last thirty minutes, completely distracted. Before Kat could respond, the door cracked open and Tristan's face appeared. His eyes darted across the room, then settled on her.

"Ready for the tour?" He nudged the door fully open with one shoulder, revealing the long lean lines of his body. A body that made her hungry to rub against it and...

Damn. Kat swallowed hard.

He wore a black V-neck sweater and dark blue jeans that hugged his legs enough to show off the muscled thighs she couldn't get out of her head. His dark hair was still slightly damp and curling at the edges. She cursed silently as her fingers twitched with the memory of how silky the thick strands of his hair had felt when she'd threaded her fingers through them and tugged.

Would she ever be able to erase the memories of their night together?

No. His voice was in her head with that low, all too seductive chuckle that melted her panties right off.

"Kat?" He rested a hand on the doorknob, staring at her.

"Sorry, I lost track of time," she muttered and carefully set her book on the bed beside her. His gaze flicked to the bed and back to her, but he didn't say a word. Tristan led her down the hall. Any stray looks at his ass were not her fault. Some men were just too...*yummy*, as her best friend Lacy would put it, to avoid gawking at them.

"I thought I'd let you see my favorite room. *This* is our library." Tristan was grinning as he opened a door that looked more like a part of the wall. Instead of a latch or a knob, a circular gold ring was set into the paneling, which could be lifted to reveal and open the "hidden" door. Tristan had to duck his head as he entered ahead of her. She gasped when she came in behind him.

The library. It was beautiful. A row of stained glass windows lined one wall. The center panel depicted St. George slaying a dragon. The two windows flanking it portrayed other scenes from the battle. The sheer mastery of the colored glass was astonishing. Such detail, the emotion on the subjects' faces, gave her goose bumps.

She moved without thinking to the center window, touching the emerald glass of the dragon's head beneath St. George's armored boot. The creature's cat-like eyes gleamed at her and seemed to be alive. It was so startling that she blinked, half afraid it might blink back. Stained glass moved Tristan to tears, just as butterflies did her. A little shiver worked up her back as she remembered him standing next to her at the bar in the Pickerel Inn pub, whispering his secret to her.

Only then did she understand what she was seeing. A little boy in this library watching the dragon, feeling small and all alone, taking heart in St. George's valiant victory. Sorrow gathered around her own heart like a black shroud. *Poor Tristan.*

"The stained glass," she whispered, and glanced at Tristan.

He was leaning against the closed library door, his focus on her. His gaze impossibly intense, a dozen emotions flashing so fast across his eyes that she couldn't figure out what he was thinking.

"Kat..." The feral desperation in his tone made Kat go very still, like a wild animal hearing a predator move past it in the underbrush. He was close to the edge, just as she was. They had to keep their distance, otherwise one of them would break and the other wouldn't be far behind.

"We can't go on like this," she whispered.

"We can't," he agreed as he came toward her. There was no stopping it, just like in the bathroom. He stopped inches from her, and that tiny space between them hummed with energy and the promise of what was to come.

She lifted her head just as he lowered his so their lips met. The scintillating caress turned molten-hot as he thrust his tongue inside to play with hers. Tristan's hands gripped her hips, tugging her flush against him. Unable to stop, her body rolled against his, and that irresistible urge to get as close to him as possible was all she could think about. He owned her with that kiss, possessed every part of her. Bursts of sexual hunger began to build in her lower abdomen, and she curled her arms around his neck, clinging to him.

He slid one hand down the back of her left thigh and lifted her leg to curl it around his hip. Kat rubbed herself against him, her mouth still locked with his. She shuddered with little bolts of pleasure as she found a way to grind herself against his muscled thigh.

"That's it," he encouraged, his voice a gruff whisper. "Ride me, love."

"Hmmm," she whimpered in excitement as she bit his bottom lip and tugged on it, playfully. It felt too good to be with him, too wicked and wonderful.

One of his hands slid down her back beneath her jeans and panties to cup one ass cheek. The sensation of his hot palm on her bare skin as he pressed her that much harder against his thigh...it was all she needed to come apart.

Sparks burst forth between them, and she kissed him savagely, gasping against him as her nerve-endings between her thighs came to life, and her clit pulsed hard enough to hurt. Her inner muscles clamped on the emptiness, and she cursed softly, wishing he'd been inside her. Panting, she sagged against him, her hands still around his neck. They'd just dry-humped like a couple of teenagers in a closet, and it wasn't enough... She could *never* get enough of Tristan.

"Steady on, darling." He nuzzled her cheek, and she could hear the smile in his voice as he simply held her close, embracing her body as it pulsed with little quivering aftershocks.

It took a minute, but when she was strong enough to stand without his help, she shoved at his chest and he stumbled back a step.

"What—"

"No, we can't, Tristan. We just..." She choked on the words. "We can't."

Her entire body vibrated with the flood of emotions. They'd already gone too far too fast. First at Fox Hill, then today in the bathroom when he'd gone down on her, and now here. There was too much fire between them, and it was going to burn them both.

She closed her eyes, blinking away the sting of tears. "I can't be with you." *It's too much of a risk, but he'll never understand. He doesn't care about me, not like I do about him. It's a game for him, and right now he's upset he's not getting what he wants. But my heart's on the line.* So much for the two of them behaving like rational adults about this.

For a long second neither of them spoke, but finally he severed eye contact and let out a slow, measured breath as though drawing in upon himself and exerting that control she didn't seem to have. Then he spun on his heel and strode across the room, back to the door. His long legs ate up the floor, putting a universe between them.

She rushed to keep up with him and, just as they both reached the door, Kat caught his arm. He glanced down at her hand, and she hastily withdrew it.

After what seemed like forever, he spoke. "Come on. I've much to show you before dinner."

Kat followed on his heels, keeping a respectable distance between them. Not that it made a difference.

He took her through the rest of the house before bringing her downstairs to the kitchen on the way to the dining room. She met the cook, Mrs. George, and a few other members of the household staff. The kitchen was a warm, cheery part of the town house, with pots hanging from a central rack over the main marble island. Fresh basil and rosemary grew in small pots on a windowsill, catching the winter sun. Kat loved how friendly Mrs. George was when she shook Kat's hand in greeting.

"So happy to meet you, dearie. Your father is quite a man, we're all happy he's here. It's been good for Elizabeth." Mrs. George's nose turned a little red, and her eyes were shining with a hint of tears.

Tristan slid an arm around her waist for a brief instant, steering her toward a plate of fresh cookies on the counter. Heat blossomed from that brief caress, and she fought the instinct to lean into him.

"Here now, Tristan, don't be eating those!" Mrs. George turned away from the ovens where she was putting in a dish that smelled of heavenly spices.

With a wicked laugh, Tristan tugged the cookie plate closer and snatched up a few, handing them over to Kat.

"Quick, lick them before Mrs. George can take them back!"

Laughing, Kat shook her head. "I'm not licking them. We're not five years old." But she did raise one Christmas tree–shaped cookie coated in green frosting to her mouth and took a bite.

The plump cook smiled indulgently at them and rolled her eyes.

"Did you get all my presents for the staff wrapped, Mrs. George?" Tristan asked as he leaned back against the counter.

With a subtle little move, he pulled Kat against his side so their bodies connected hip to hip. His scent tickled Kat's nose and heat rushed to her cheeks.

It was so easy to pretend that this was natural, that they were a couple, enjoying a Christmas in the kitchen, eating cookies, sharing smiles, excited about being alone together later. A fierce ache rose up inside her like a howling wind, filling her with despair. This wasn't to be; it was an impossible fantasy, and she shouldn't let herself even pretend that life could be this wonderful. The ghosts of their pain in the library were momentarily banished as she let herself pretend she could have this wonderful dream.

"I did get them wrapped! Thank you, Tristan. The maids will love their new fur-lined gloves." The cook grinned. "And of course, I had a peek at mine. You shouldn't have bought that knitting set."

"Nonsense, Mrs. George. How am I to get a new scarf every year if you don't have the tools to make one?" He winked at the cook, who just laughed.

"Off with you now, and don't let your mother see you eating my cookies."

Tristan curled his arm around Kat's hips as he led her out of the kitchen. Kat didn't protest or try to move his hand, even though she knew she shouldn't let him touch her like that. It was a risk. They could be seen...but she wanted that contact badly enough to risk it.

She and Tristan were almost behaving normally, not like two people who wanted desperately to sleep together but couldn't. It should've been a relief, but instead a hollowness was steadily growing inside her chest.

"Is it normal for someone like your mom to have servants?" Kat asked Tristan. "I mean, she isn't married to an earl anymore..."

Several gold frames covered the walls of the main hall, the

art within depicting men and women from different eras, posing for the artists. Kat couldn't help but admire that—having one's ancestors captured in oil paintings. She and her father only had a few grainy snapshots of great-grandparents in front of log cabins.

"Mum needs them to help out, and most women of her status have a couple of servants. At my father's estate the staff is three times as large. He doesn't need them all, but he's rather traditional," Tristan explained.

"Oh." She followed him as they entered the dining hall.

Three tall windows let evening sun in, warming the walnut of the dining-room table. A glass chandelier above the table glittered, casting sparkles of light against the walls. Kat noticed the pale green walls, which had tree branches and vines with blooming flowers painted on them. If she ignored the snow outside, she could pretend she was in a forest.

"Oh, it's beautiful." She sighed.

Tristan's lips twitched, but the expression was fleeting. "I'm glad it meets with your approval."

"Tristan..."

Before she could say anything else, their parents strolled in, arm in arm, laughing and smiling. At the sight of their kids, they dropped their arms.

"Hey honey, did you get a chance to see the rest of the house?" Her dad grinned and walked over to her, trapping her in a strong hug.

Kat nodded and with a little nervous flutter she spoke to Lizzy. "Your house is beautiful."

A blush stained Lizzy's cheeks, and she smiled shyly. "Thank you. I want you to feel at home here."

Lizzy's genuine heartfelt response warmed Kat inside.

"I hope Tristan told you some of the history of the house?" Lizzy said as she gestured for everyone to sit. They picked the far end of the large table, making dining more intimate.

"Yes, he did." Kat tensed as Tristan placed a hand on her lower back and guided her to a chair across from his mother. That single touch, so intimate, so familiar, sent little shivers through her body and burned her skin with memories of the other times he'd touched her. She already knew with a sinking heart that she was going to miss being with Tristan. And not just physically. The way she felt around him, like anything was possible, and she could go out and take risks—all of that might vanish, too. And she didn't want it to.

Kat glanced at Tristan as he pulled her chair out for her and then scooted it in when she sat down. Tristan's expression was contemplative, but his eyes betrayed nothing of his thoughts.

Her father sat down next to Lizzy, and Tristan chose the seat next to Kat. His chair was too close to hers, but neither of their parents seemed to notice. Their knees were almost touching, and she wanted that contact so badly; her whole body silently begged her, with little sparks and flashes of heat, to get even closer to him so he could set her ablaze.

Have to stay in control. Can't let him know how much I want to touch him, to rub my cheek on his shoulder and breathe in his scent. Tristan was addictive, but she couldn't let herself take another hit. Forcing her thoughts away from Tristan—not that she was entirely successful—

she turned her attention back to their parents.

It was almost comical, the adults facing their kids across the table. But there was no way she could laugh right now. Not when Tristan's leg was pressing against hers from knee to hip. Heat emanated from her leg where it touched his, and yet she couldn't bear to move away.

It was impossible for her to deny herself these small touches.

Sometimes a girl can't help herself...

So she kept her leg where it was but didn't dare look his way.

"So..." her father said, breaking the awkward silence. "What's on the menu for tonight?" He caught Kat's eye and patted his stomach. "I've gotten spoiled by Mrs. George." Despite his words, Kat could tell he was still healthy and fit.

"Well." Lizzy clasped her hands together. "Mrs. George wanted an Indian theme night after Clayton said you both liked Indian food. Tikka masala and kedgeree are on the menu, as well as spiced beef tongue."

Beef tongue? Kat did love Indian food, but she drew the line at tongues of animals.

"Sounds...great," she said, swallowing down the urge to gag. *Ugh*. This was going to be a nightmare.

As the footman brought in plates of tikka masala and a basket of naan bread, Kat decided she'd fill up on these items first and see if she could avoid the tongue.

"Lizzy, I thought we might go to a concert on New Year's Eve. The London Symphony has a wonderful Chopin arrangement planned," her father suggested.

"What a wonderful idea," Lizzy replied, passing the naan basket toward her and Tristan

Kat lost track of what they were saying when Tristan put an arm around the back of her chair. Then he lazily leaned forward to hook a finger around the edge of the basket of naan, dragging it closer to them.

"You don't have to eat everything, you know," he murmured, just loud enough for her to hear.

"What?" she muttered, hating that she had to lean closer

to him to do it. That intoxicating Tristan scent enveloped her and made her a little dizzy.

"The tongue. You went white as ash when Mum mentioned it. You don't *have* to eat it." He nudged the naan in front of her and waited patiently for her to collect two pieces and set them on her plate. Then he took some for himself and pushed the basket toward their parents. As he did this, he removed his arm from her chair and brushed his hand against her arm, then her hip as he lowered it back beneath the table. It took everything inside her to keep from jerking as her body responded to the electric tingles from that contact.

"Kat." Lizzy caught her attention. "Your father tells me you love history?"

Kat scooted forward in her chair and nodded, relieved to have someone to talk to besides Tristan and a safe topic with which to distract herself. "Yes, I'm getting my degree in it."

"That's wonderful! What do you see yourself doing after you finish your program?" Lizzy sipped her wine and leaned toward the table.

"She's hoping to teach someday, be a professor," Tristan cut in, then froze. He'd spoken so naturally, as though he'd been settling into the pleasant atmosphere of the dinner. But he'd forgotten one thing: He wasn't supposed to know *anything* about her. Not her hopes and dreams, just as she wasn't supposed to know his.

We must be polite strangers. Not people whose souls have touched.

Kat swallowed the lump of panic in her throat. "Er...yes. I was telling Tristan during the tour that I'd love to be a college professor and teach history classes."

Her father and Lizzy shared bemused looks before Tristan's mother spoke. "Well, I'm so glad you two have had a chance to get to know each other. London is full of history. Have you had a chance to take in the sights?"

"She hasn't." Her father cut in and winked not-so-subtly at Lizzy. "Wouldn't it be nice if someone showed her around while she's here for the holidays?"

"Yes!" Lizzy's exclamation was a little too eager as she replied to Clayton. "Tristan thought he might have a chance to show Kat around since you and I will be busy with wedding arrangements." She turned to Kat, beaming. "You two can get better acquainted."

"Yes, I'd be delighted to take Kat around London." He turned his focus her way. His body emanated a subtle heat, reminding her just how close they were. "Well, what do you say? A bit of tourism to appease the parents?" His tone was light, teasing, but damned if his eyes weren't burning hot in a way that made her flush all over.

She'd once been afraid of their fire, of the way their passion sparked things, dark delicious things inside her. Now she missed it, craved it like she'd never craved anything else. He was keeping his distance, though, because she was terrified of getting her heart broken.

"I'm in." Kat's voice was strong and clear as she met his gaze with her own.

It was all so frustrating and confusing. She was crazy for holding him at arm's length but still wanting to be around him. She knew it would only end badly. Kat refused to be the only one suffering from repressing whatever it was that kept sparking between them. He was torturing her with those lingering glances, and the gentle, familiar caresses, as though he wanted to drive her mad with the memories of how wonderful it had been between them.

He's killing me with his tempting sweetness.

The little devil that perched on her shoulder whispered an irresistible suggestion. *"Show him you can play the game, too."*

Dropping one of her hands beneath the table, she

brushed the tips of her fingers against his upper thigh and then placed her palm against his leg.

Clink!

Tristan's fork struck the china plate, and his entire body went rigid. She pulled her hand away, pretending to fiddle with her thick cloth napkin. After several deep breaths, he picked up his fork again, not looking at her.

"Tristan, everything all right?" her father asked.

"Yes," he ground out, his voice slightly rough. Her father's brows rose, and he shared a concerned glance with Lizzy.

"So, Kat, any dashing young men at Cambridge catch your attention?" Lizzy asked.

With a sputtered cough, Kat swallowed her bite of tikka masala. She lunged for her water glass, desperate to wash down her dinner so she could catch her breath. A faint, muffled snicker came from her left. She could practically hear Tristan's rich, accented voice in her head, teasing her.

"Well done, Kitty-Kat, can you make it any more obvious?"

She shot him a vengeful look, her heart beating wildly. In an attempt to pay him back for that snicker, she reached for his leg again, but had to stifle a gasp when he caught her hand and placed it high up on his inner thigh, moving it slowly toward his groin. An explosion of heat made her face feel as though it were on fire. He wouldn't let go of her hand.

"Kat?" Her father was staring at her, frowning.

She hadn't answered Lizzy. Swallowing again, she cleared her throat. "I'm not dating anyone, but there was someone..." She paused, choosing her words carefully. Under the table, Tristan still clasped her hand against his thigh. The initial bruising hold softened, and his thumb began to rub in a slow smoothing motion against the rapidly beating pulse point on her inner wrist. An ache settled deep in her chest at that gentle reminder of his ability to affect her.

"Someone?" Her father straightened in his chair, his eyes filled with curiosity.

"Hmmm?" She met her dad's gaze but tried to control her reaction.

Was it hot in here?

She couldn't breathe. She wasn't good at deception or lying. And even if she had been, her father was overprotective. It wouldn't matter if she were sixteen or nineteen; he would still be watchful over her with any man she dated. If he knew she was talking about Tristan, he'd probably post himself outside her door, a shotgun slung loose over one arm, ready to use it on any sexy British playboy that might attempt to sneak into her bedroom under the cover of darkness.

"Just make sure that you're finding time to study."

With a slow, precise movement of defiance, she set her fork down and glared at her father. "It doesn't matter. It was over before it began."

And just like that, Tristan's hand was gone. Her skin instantly cooled without his warm touch. She moved her hand back to her lap. For a second she thought her father would respond, but he held his tongue and took a sip of his wine.

"What about you, Tristan? Are you planning on seeing anyone over the holidays, say Brianna Wolverton?" Lizzy asked.

Kat tried not to react, but she couldn't help shooting a glance at Tristan. She did her best to look only mildly interested, like a new stepsister would—not like the girl Tristan had made love to a few days ago, before everything had gone to hell. Her heart pounded hard against her rib cage, and it made everything in her chest hurt.

"Alas, no, Mum. I've been focused on my studies, which must take precedence over romance." His tone was teasing and light, but Kat didn't miss the way his jaw clenched after he'd spoken.

"I thought that you and Brianna might be back together after what I saw in the *Daily Mail*," Lizzy observed. "I wish they wouldn't put your picture in those terrible newspapers just to make a fuss whenever your father is vocal in Parliament." Shame and embarrassment mixed with anger seemed to pulse off Lizzy, and her porcelain skin grew pink. Her fingers flipped a napkin about, twiddling it on the table until Kat's father leaned over and put a hand over Lizzy's, stilling her.

"Don't let it bother you, sweetheart. The paparazzi follow Tristan because it's the best way to upset his father's political involvement. You can't let it get to you."

"I know," she whispered. "But it isn't fair that they target Tristan."

While this entire exchange went on, Kat kept sneaking glances at Tristan. He was stone-faced and silent, his hand curled into a menacing fist by his plate. A tic worked in his jaw as he stared straight ahead at something she couldn't see.

"Pardon me." He suddenly shoved his chair back from the table. "I've lost my appetite." Just like that, without another word, he stalked from the room.

"Trist—" Lizzy started to say, but Kat's father cut her off.

"Let him go, sweetheart. It must be tough for him to deal with his father, the tabloids, and now us."

Lizzy nodded shakily, but managed a brave smile. "I know. We knew this would be hard, and I wish there was a way to make it all easier."

Watching her father and Tristan's mother holding hands, comforting each other, made Kat's chest squeeze. She needed a minute alone, herself, and she felt she ought to give the parents a moment alone, too. She didn't bother to excuse herself; she just dashed from the dining room.

Fleeing up the first set of stairs, she paused at the top of the landing. The media room door was ajar. It had a large, black *L*-shaped sofa facing a massive flat-screen TV and bookshelves that stretched from floor to ceiling on either side of it. Kat tiptoed up to the door and peered inside. Tristan stood by the TV, turning on a music station with a small remote. A composer's name came up on the screen, a name she recognized. Rachmaninoff. Her favorite composer. With a little twinge of guilt, she lingered there, out of sight, watching him as he turned on the music.

I should walk away, leave him alone. Logically, that's what she should do, but she couldn't. The music swelled out of the speakers in a powerful, emotional sound wave that drew her into the room. Tristan braced his hands on the ledge of a bookshelf and dropped his head, his shoulders sagging. He looked so...tired.

"Tristan," Kat said, so softly she was surprised when he glanced over his shoulder at her.

"Not now, Kat. I'm not in a good mood." The subtle warning in his tone went unheeded.

She didn't want to leave him, and she didn't want to sit alone in her room, hating herself for this whole stupid situation. The last few months she'd been craving an adventure and now she couldn't experience the adventure that called to her most. She didn't want to risk her father finding out, but she was more scared that she'd fall in love with Tristan.

The night she'd agreed to be with him, she'd convinced herself that she could enjoy him and not worry about what tomorrow would bring. Yet tomorrow had come, and she was facing the consequences of losing him. Falling in love with him was too dangerous an adventure for her. Heartbreak was not on the list of things she ever wanted to experience.

Still, she stood there, so close to him, unable to walk away.

"Don't send me away."

He dropped a hand to his side and finally looked at her.

"I'm not a bloody saint, Kat. If I stay here with you..." His eyes were almost feral with hunger and desperation. "I won't be able to stay away, not in the way you want. This thing between us, it burns too hot. I want to take you to my bed and never let you leave. The things I want to do to you..." Tristan stepped back and raked a hand through his dark hair, tugging the strands as he blew out a ragged breath.

"The things I want to do to you..." The words made her shiver with excitement. She knew just what sort of bad, dirty, and explosive things he could do to her and she knew she'd love every minute of it. Because it was *him*, her beautiful British bad boy, the one who knew her secrets, the one she'd let get dangerously close to her heart.

"Don't test me. We both know I can seduce you. Just one touch..." His right hand lifted as though to cup her face, but he paused, then dropped his hand, his face contorted with frustration.

He's not angry at me. He's angry that he can't have me. Just like I'm upset I can't have him.

Her skin tingled where he would have touched her, as though it had felt his phantom caress. That little voice inside her head whispered for her to move closer, to encourage him to touch her.

The first one to cave would drag the other into trouble. It would only take one wrong touch, one teasing kiss, and they'd be up against the wall, breathless and panting.

"Fucking hell." He shouldered past her, leaving the room.

I'm an idiot. Because she'd let him walk away. Because she'd wanted him, and it was going to destroy them both.

Her heart froze to stone in her chest with every step he took and she couldn't help but follow him as he left the media room.

He descended the main stairs, walked past the dining room where her father and Lizzy were still having dinner, and snatched his black coat from the coatrack in the entranceway. He slung it on and dug around in his pockets for his keys.

Throwing open the front door, he paused. "If you really want there to be nothing between us, stay far away from me." His voice was low, soft enough that they're parents wouldn't overhear from the dining room.

He met her gaze. "Now that I've had you once, I crave you like I've never craved anyone else. Don't test my fraying control."

Kat's knees buckled, and she clutched the banister as she watched him storm out into the snowy night. A second after the door slammed shut, she sank to the floor, sitting on the bottom stair. The cool wood spindles of the railing pressed hard against her cheek as she sat there, hating how badly she wanted to leave with him.

I have to keep my distance, even though we're stuck together for the holidays.

Would his mother still make him show her around London? How would they cope with having to be so close? She would have to summon nerves of steel to withstand the building tide of emotions.

I can't fall in love with Tristan Kingsley.

❧ 6 ❧

Tristan leaned over the bar to take his third pint of Guinness from the bartender at the Stowaway Pub. It was one of his few haunts that the paparazzi hadn't discovered yet. Partially because it wasn't the sort of place they expected him to go. He usually dined at the best restaurants, frequented the most expensive clubs, but here, in this tiny, backdoor establishment, he could be what the name suggested: a stowaway, content to have a pint in peace.

"Thank you," he said, nodding at the bartender before turning back to the pub's crowded room. Despite the snow, Londoners had flooded the small, warm, wood confines of the pub. He ignored the rowdy occupants and tipped his glass back.

What a wretched day. To have Kat under his roof and not be able to touch her was killing him. When they'd been in the bathroom together, he'd been so close to seducing her. He'd seen that look in her eyes, so full of a hunger that matched his own, but she was fighting the attraction between them.

I could keep it a secret. It would even be fun... But Kat wasn't a secretive girl. She was open and honest, every emotion showing on her face. Their parents would figure it out sooner or later, and the game would be over.

She was more than an itch to scratch. If she were, it would be easy enough to move on. But she was an *obsession*, and if he didn't regain his control, he'd push too fast and ruin his plans to have her. His mother expected him to take Kat around London over the holidays. He was happy to have more time with her, but he knew it would be a test for him to be on his best behavior. Or at least the best he could manage, because he couldn't hide how much he still wanted her.

It was going to be hell.

I'll play by her rules, but that doesn't mean I won't fight dirty to get her back in my bed. He was a master at slow seduction, with caresses, little knowing smiles, a brush of lips... He would make it impossible for Kat to resist him.

"Hello, Tristan." A feminine voice halted his deep drinking.

He slowly lowered his hand, peering through the froth-coated glass at Brianna Wolverton. She was wearing a long, white wool coat and sleek black pants. Even in slushy winter weather, Brianna had flair. She'd pulled her pale blonde hair back in a fashionably messy ponytail, and she was studying him curiously

"Brianna." He chuckled. The ale was relaxing him, and he didn't mind her companionship. Their friendship stretched back years.

"Carter said you might be in London for the holidays." Her eyes darted around the room. "The chances of you coming to the Stowaway were in my favor." A knowing smile played on her lips. She knew him well. It was the nearest pub to his mother's town house, and they'd often met here for drinks before having a bit of fun.

"How are you?" Tristan asked, raising his pint in a salute to his former paramour.

With a little *tsk*-ing noise, she stole his pint and drank the rest of it, then plopped the glass down on the bar beside him.

"I'm fine, thank you. How many have you had, Tristan?" She nudged the empty glass with an elegant fingertip, her eyes full of concern. They'd both lived wild lives, but they'd always watched each other's backs, too.

"Not nearly enough," he growled and started to turn back to the bar again, but a hand gripped his arm.

"It has been a long time since I've seen you like this. Tell me, what's the matter?" Without waiting for an answer, Brianna tugged him through the crowds to a small table out of the way. Tristan let her shove him into a chair.

Brianna nudged his shin with her booted toe. "Talk, Kingsley. What's your father done this time?" she asked. "Was it the photo of us? I saw that. I can't believe someone spotted us in that mew. We were well hidden." A little frown tugged her full lips down.

Tristan scowled. Another fortune tossed at the papers to silence the rumors of his love life. He was surprised his father hadn't called to berate him.

"No, it's not my father. It's my mum, sort of." He grumbled and eyed the bar counter where the barkeep was filling up more pints.

Bloody hell, I want to forget tonight.

"Your mum?" Brianna's eyes widened. "Oh dear, what's happened?"

He laughed bitterly. "Where to start? She's engaged to an American investment banker, and I'm inheriting a stepsister. The worst part is that I've just met the loveliest young woman who" he paused, tailoring his words— "was absolutely stunning in bed."

Brianna nibbled her bottom lip. "Wait a moment, that's an awful lot to take in. Let's start with the first part. Your mum is getting married? To an American? I'm sure your father doesn't like that."

With a shrug of his shoulder, Tristan replied, "I don't believe he knows yet."

"Then we won't worry about your father finding out until he does. Now, what's wrong with the woman you're interested in? Last time I checked, being good in bed was a *good* thing."

He propped his elbow on the table and smashed the heels of his palms into his eyes, trying to black out the ever-present visions of Kat that kept taunting and torturing him.

"The young woman in question happens to be my new *stepsister*."

Brianna's lips parted. "Ballocks." She so rarely cursed, it made him bark out a hoarse laugh. "You're shagging your stepsister? And she's American? Oh dear, this *is* bad." She leaned forward and whispered, "What will happen when you father finds out?" Her eyes flicked around to the nearest tables as though expecting the paps to pop out and flash their cameras. It wouldn't have been the first time.

"*Shagged*, as in one night. And she isn't my stepsister just yet. We met before we knew our parents were dating. We got together at a party at the end of term, then went our separate ways for the break, which happened to be in the same place. My mother's town house. Mum had some brilliant idea we could all get to know each other over holiday." He dropped his arms to the table and covered his face with his hands.

Brianna waved over a waiter. "Two more pints of Guinness, please." Then she turned back to him. "You're right, you do need another. I take it things are awkward since you've had her and now don't want her. Is she one of those clingy women?"

He shook his head. In the past he almost never slept with a woman twice, Brianna being the exception. But that was because neither of them expected or wanted it to go past the bedroom.

"No, she's the one who called it off. I wanted...more. But when she realized the situation could potentially put our parents' nuptials at risk, she broke it off." He picked up the new beer that the waiter had set in front of him and chugged it down, not caring that the room spun a little as he did so. The fact that he'd had four pints before Brianna arrived wasn't good.

His friend watched him while she took a small sip of her own drink. "*You* want more?" She seemed to test the word, as though she'd never spoken it before and it was foreign to her.

"Yes." Hell, he didn't know what he wanted, except he knew he wanted Kat. Wanted more than the two nights he'd had with her.

"Tristan, do you realize how insane that sounds?" It was clear from Brianna's wide, disbelieving eyes that she didn't grasp the seriousness of this situation.

"I'm in a bloody nightmare, Bri. You have to help me." He reached across the table and clasped her hand. Her gaze dropped to the table, then lifted again, her mouth forming a little *O*-shape that used to make him hard and aching to fuck it. But he didn't see the appeal anymore. There was only Kat, Kat's mouth, Kat's lips, Kat's little smile, her laugh, the way she hummed Russian symphonies when she thought he wasn't paying attention.

"Darling, you have it bad," Brianna cooed with sympathy. "It's all over your face. You can't get her out of your head."

He nodded. No point in denying it.

"Can't you seduce her? No woman can deny you when you turn on your charm."

He puffed out a slow breath. "She made me swear to leave her alone."

Brianna giggled. "My, my, a woman who can turn *you* down. I'd like to meet this little stepsister of yours."

"No!" he sputtered. "She's seen the photos of us. Our history...it almost made me lose her once before because she thought I'd cheated on her. I can't go through that again." When she'd accused him of cheating on her and demanded that he never see her again, it had nearly broken him. A thing he'd never thought possible. But the thought of never seeing Kat again, never kissing her, never talking to her late into the night...it had been unbearable. He'd explained the pictures to Kat, how he and Brianna had been together a few weeks before he'd met Kat, but the papers printed pictures whenever they felt like it. It had taken her almost two weeks to finally accept what he'd told her. That he *hadn't* cheated on her.

"Hmm..." Brianna pursed her lips thoughtfully and nudged his pint at him again. "Drink up and tell me more about her."

Tristan drank the pint and another as he told Brianna everything he knew about Katherine Roberts, from her love of history to her crying over monarch butterflies.

"She cries over butterflies? Why?" Brianna slid a third pint to him. When had that one shown up? He'd apparently lost count. His hands felt a little weak, and his brain a tad fuzzy, but he closed his fingers around the pint.

"Because they're dying out. She used to see hundreds when she was a child. Now she's lucky to see even one." The sudden wave of depression hit him. "It *is* sad, isn't it?" he said, his speech slurred and his tongue a little thicker than he remembered.

"I think you've had enough." Brianna's voice seemed to come through a heavy fog.

"*Yes.*" He dragged out the word as everything around him went black.

⚜

BRIANNA WOLVERTON STARED AT THE UNCONSCIOUS MAN on the opposite side of the table.

"Sorry, Tristan, but you'll thank me later." She pulled out her cellphone and dialed a number.

"Hello?" A deep voice came through.

"Carter, it's Brianna. I've got Tristan at the Stowaway. Can you come by and take him home?"

"Er..."

The rustle of clothes and a feminine giggle came through the phone line before he replied.

"Of course. Give me five minutes. I'm not far." Carter disconnected the call.

Brianna pocketed her phone and resumed drinking her beer.

"He okay, love?" The barkeep walked over and gave Tristan's shoulder a gentle shove.

"He's fine. Had a long day, and the last pint dropped him like a stone."

"Uh-huh." The man grunted and wandered off.

Less than five minutes later, Carter strolled into the pub, his blond hair a rough mess, and Brianna almost laughed. At least someone had gotten fucked in a good way tonight.

Carter noticed her and strode over, frowning as he saw his best friend half asleep, his face resting on his arms on the table. "What's the matter with him?"

"I might've slipped him a heavy dose of allergy medicine. It made him a little drowsy."

"What? Why the bloody hell would you do that, Bri?"

She rolled one shoulder in a shrug. "Because he needs to be

63

vulnerable tonight." If they could get Tristan home to Kat while he was a little out of it, he might open up to her, show that soft-hearted core he worked so hard to hide, and Kat wouldn't be able to turn him down. Maybe, just maybe, he could escape his father's control and have a life he wanted with a girl he wanted. She cared enough about Tristan to help him take the risk.

Maybe then, there would be hope for me.

"Bri..." Carter growled. "You aren't making sense."

"Actually," she said, pushing her chair back and standing, "I'm a genius. Help me get him to your car, he's awake enough to walk. I'll explain along the way."

☙❧

KAT COULDN'T SLEEP. KNOWING TRISTAN WAS SOMEWHERE out in the night, doing Lord knew what because she'd pushed him away... Her stomach roiled, and she curled up in the leather armchair in the library.

A sudden scuffling noise followed by a grunt and a low curse outside the library jerked her out of the chair. She rushed to the doorway and gasped. Tristan was stumbling down the hall, one arm slung over another man's shoulder.

It was the same tall, blond-haired man who'd given her the Fox Hill party invitation. Without a thought, Kat left the library and went to meet them.

"What happened? Is he okay?" She took hold of Tristan's other arm and helped the man carry him to Tristan's room. Once they got him inside, he collapsed on his bed, eyes half-open and a little dazed as he stared up at them.

"He drank too much," the man explained in a low voice.

"Too much?" She sucked in a breath. "Do we need to take him to the hospital?"

With a shake of his head, he tossed his hair out of his

eyes. "No hospital. The press always gets wind of that sort of thing. He'll be fine. But someone will need to watch him for the next several hours in case he gets sick."

"Aren't you staying?" she asked.

He shook his head. "Wish I could, but I can't. I'm Carter, by the way. I don't believe we've officially met." He held out a hand and Kat shook it.

"I'm Katherine Roberts. Everyone just calls me 'Kat.'"

"Kat." Carter laughed. "So *you* are Tristan's future stepsister?"

How did he know? She shifted restlessly on her bare feet. She was in her pajamas, and Carter's intense focus made her feel a little vulnerable.

"Er...yes."

The fine lines at the corners of his eyes crinkled as he smiled. "You're one of the undergraduates from the Fox Hill party. I thought you looked familiar."

Managing a nod, she smiled faintly. "Yeah, I was with my friend Lacy."

He made a little noise that sounded like a stifled snicker as he turned his attention back to Tristan.

"We should get him out of his clothes. He'll be angry if he sleeps in them," Carter said.

"What?" Undress Tristan? That was a terrible idea. Terrible. The last thing she needed was a reason to put her hands on all those smooth, hard muscles...such a bad idea.

"Come on, help me." Carter started to lift Tristan up, and Kat moved to assist on the other side. They pulled off his coat and then his sweater.

The movement must have roused Tristan, because he grinned a little and stared at her.

"Kitty-Kat, *my* Kat." His sensual, albeit slightly slurred purr made her wince, and made Carter laugh a little louder.

"That's right, ol' boy, your Kitty-Kat." Carter shot her a grin and winked at her.

"My Kat," Tristan whispered, more sweetly, his eyelids dropping. His near helplessness made something inside her curl up and want to purr right back. But she had to take care of him; he was clearly way too drunk to be left alone.

She worked alongside Carter until they got him down to his trousers.

"That's as far as I'll go. You can handle it from here, Kat." Carter started to back away.

"Hey wait! I can't take his pants off!" she hissed so as not to be overhead by the parents down the hall.

"You have to, those are expensive trousers. If he throws up on those, he'll be furious tomorrow." Carter tossed a slim black smartphone on the bed. "I'm in his contacts if you need me. I'm staying nearby." He headed for the door.

"Carter!" she whispered loud enough for him to hear, but he didn't stop. He exited the bedroom, leaving her alone with a half-naked Tristan.

Great. Just great. This is exactly what I need tonight.

She pivoted around to face Tristan, who was leaning against one of the posts at the end of the bed.

With a slow movement, he reached up to catch a lock of her hair.

"Lovely." He sighed dreamily and tugged the lock gently. "Missed you, did I tell you?" he said, his words still slurred and a little wistful.

Kat carefully removed her hair from around his finger, fighting the warmth that his confession made her feel.

If I let him win me over like this...

"We're leaving the pants on, that better be okay with you," she muttered. Then more loudly she said, "Do you need some water or something?"

He nodded, blinking. "Water, yes."

She stepped back and held a hand up to his chest, touching him firmly.

"Stay right there. I'll get you a glass of water from the kitchen." Then she dashed out of the bedroom and down the stairs, trying to muffle her steps as best she could. It was nearly two in the morning, and Kat didn't think their parents would be pleased to wake up because Tristan was drunk.

When she got back to his room with the water, he wasn't sitting on the bed. Her heart jumped into her throat as she scanned the room. Where had he gone? Hopefully not somewhere else in the house.

The sounds of retching came from the bathroom down the hall.

She found him on his knees, one forearm braced on the toilet seat as he dry heaved. His eyes were closed, and he was breathing so hard he was panting. Beads of sweat gathered on his forehead.

"Tristan! Are you okay?" Kat got down on her knees beside him and rubbed a hand over his back.

Her palm heated the instant she touched his warm skin, and she could feel the muscles leaping and twitching beneath her palm as he heaved again.

The tendons in his neck turned taut for several long seconds before he relaxed, gasping softly. He rested his forehead on his arm and didn't move for a while except to catch his breath.

Kat stayed there, hurting with him. She rested her cheek on his bare shoulder and trailed her fingertips lightly along his skin, soothing him as best she could. It was something her father used to do whenever Kat had been suffering from the stomach flu. He would sit beside her just like this, offering comfort.

After about ten minutes had passed, and Tristan hadn't heaved again, she stroked her fingers through his hair.

"I feel...better," he ground out in a gruff whisper. "May I have the glass of water and some mouthwash?"

"Sure." She reached for the glass she'd set on the bathroom counter and held it out to him, then retrieved the mouthwash, too.

He pushed away from the toilet and took the glass, gulping down every last drop before he set it on the tile floor. Then he tipped back the bottle of mouthwash and swished it around for several seconds before he swallowed.

"I don't think you're supposed to—"

"Can't have that taste in my mouth," he muttered with an exhausted sigh. "Thank you." When he glanced at her, the knot of anxiety in her chest eased. Tenderness was reflected back at her through those blue-green eyes.

She hadn't realized how much she needed to see that, his affection for her still burning in his gaze.

He still wants me.

"You're welcome." Kat kept hold of his shoulder, and neither of them looked away.

How did I think I could just turn off my feelings? Because I'm an idiot. She mentally shook herself. They had to stay away from each other, but it was clear now that what she felt wasn't going away, not anytime soon.

Tristan tensed as he gripped the edge of the counter and hauled himself up. He stumbled a step, as though his legs couldn't quite hold him up.

She reacted instantly, catching him by the waist. He didn't hesitate to curl an arm around her, using her strength for support. He was so tall, muscled, and strong, yet in this moment, he needed her.

No one had ever *needed* her before. A secret emotion she didn't want to confront began to pulse and glow with warmth inside her chest. It seemed he needed her as much as she needed him. He had so much of the world at his fingertips compared to her, but he made her feel like she was the one thing he truly wanted.

As they walked back to his room, she relished the way they seemed to hold on to each other more than just physically. The connection that drew them together was hard to break, and tonight, she couldn't leave him alone.

"Do you need help getting into bed?" Just asking the question made her mouth run dry.

Tristan leaned against one bedpost and stared down at himself, then shook his head.

"No," he said and, with a staggering few steps, collapsed onto the bed.

Kat walked to the open bedroom doorway and lingered, watching his body as he shifted and then rolled onto his back on the bed. *If he's that drunk, someone should look after him. Just because we can't be lovers doesn't mean I can't care for him when he needs me.*

His head turned her way, and the dim light from the hallway illuminated his eyes, making them spark and sparkle like diamonds shot through with electricity.

"You don't have to stay," he whispered.

Sighing, Kat closed the door, sealing them in darkness before she padded over to him and climbed onto his big bed. She lay down next to him

"I want to stay. Get some rest."

She shivered. There was something impossibly intimate about two bodies in a bed, darkness cloaking them as they whispered to each other. It was as though she and Tristan were the last two people on earth, no secrets, no games between them. Just a shared presence in the dark of night.

He was silent, but after a long second, his body moved toward hers, and she tensed, expecting him to try to seduce her. All he did was wrap himself around her and press a kiss to her neck as he nuzzled his face in her hair. Tristan tucked his head into the crook of her shoulder. Warm breath fanned her skin, and his body heated hers as he held on to her from behind, their bodies curved like a pair of spoons. How could sleeping with him, *just sleeping* be so calming and wonderful?

It felt right.

Don't think about tomorrow.

❧ 7 ☙

ucking hell.

A headache slammed against his temples so hard it made his stomach turn over.

The only thing that wasn't hell was having Kat in his arms when he woke up.

It was pure *heaven*. She felt so good, her lush curves pressed against him, the scent of her floral shampoo clinging to the rich brown locks of her hair, which he wanted to wrap around his fist as he tugged her head back for a kiss. He buried his face in her hair, inhaling that feminine scent. How could she smell so delicious? He wanted to devour her, to taste her in so many places, to imprint her scent and taste upon himself so he could never forget it. Yet, what he felt was deeper, too, had always been, it seemed, from the moment he'd met her. Tristan couldn't shake the thought that he would never want another woman again, not after having Kat in his life.

He pressed his lips to her neck. She didn't even stir—out like a light, bless her. She was so...

He blinked and froze.

What was Kat doing in his bed? Last night they'd argued...the memories were blurry and tinged with gaping blank spots. He did remember how awkward dinner had been, the revenge game their hands had played beneath the table. Then he was drinking...with Brianna.

Brianna. Pain shot through his skull and his eyeballs. He shut his eyes, and lifted a hand to his head, rubbing at his temples as he stifled a groan of agony. After Brianna, he couldn't remember anything except a vague notion that he'd spent part of the night bent over a toilet, retching like a young pup after his first pint. He'd had too many, but that wasn't new. Having a black spot in his memory was not good. He was going to have a chat with Brianna soon.

But first he had to deal with Kat. He had to get her back into her own bed before their parents discovered they'd slept together the night before. Kat had been right, as much as he didn't want to admit it. If they got caught, it would devastate his mother and her father. He loved his mother and didn't want to hurt her. He knew Clayton would be furious if he realized Tristan was sleeping with his daughter.

Frowning, he forced himself to sit up in his bed and let go of Kat. He was shirtless, she in her pajamas. It didn't look like they'd done anything except sleep. Tristan was thankful for that, but only because he wanted to remember every night with her, and losing a memory was infuriating.

He glanced at the clock on the nightstand. Six a.m. With a low curse, Tristan climbed out of bed and walked around to Kat's side.

Scooping her up in his arms, he carried her down the hall to her room and deposited her on her bed. She'd likely lost sleep last night when he'd come home, and he wanted to make sure she got enough rest. He pulled back the covers and slid her beneath the sheets. She barely stirred, murmuring something soft and unintelligible before nuzzling her pillow and drifting back to sleep.

That strange heat filled his chest again, hot as arousal but not the same—something just as potent and mystifying, but tempered with a fondness he couldn't explain. Tristan leaned over and kissed her cheek. Never in his life had he kissed a woman who wasn't awake, or without a purpose to seduce her.

This kiss was different. It came from a need deep inside him to connect with her, to show her, even in her sleep, that he cared about her.

I know I shouldn't. Too bloody dangerous. But I do. God help me, I do.

He tucked the blankets around her and turned off the lights before he closed the door and walked down the hall to the bathroom. Cranking the handles, he turned on the hot water in the shower. Then he stripped out of his clothes and got in. The hiss of the water on the tile and the feel of it on his skin relaxed his tense muscles. He braced an arm on the wall and leaned his head against it, letting the burn of the shower sizzle against his skin.

Tristan tried to resurrect moments from the previous night, but they slipped off into the corners of his mind like fractured shadows, twisting away, eluding him every time he reached for them. They left him empty, shaking, and still a little nauseous. But one thing was clear: He had to decide what he was going to do about Kat. Dancing around each other and their undeniable attraction would not end well.

After his shower, he headed down to the kitchen. It was nearly seven a.m., unusually early for him, but there was little point in going back to his own bed alone.

"Tristan." Clayton's pleasant greeting halted him in his tracks. "Have a good night's sleep?" Kat's father sat at a small nook table, sipping from a white coffee mug.

Tristan's heartbeat spiked, and the sudden tension in his shoulders made his neck hurt. He tried to relax. There was no way Clayton could know Kat had spent the night with him. Tristan debated answering the question. He couldn't tell the truth.

I slept well, considering I held your daughter in my arms, dreaming of all the ways I want to take her in my bed. That wouldn't go over well.

"Well enough. You?" he asked as he walked over to the stove to heat water for tea.

"Fine." Clayton flattened his paper on the table and sat back in his chair, crossing his arms over his chest.

Tristan almost smiled.

A lesser man would have felt threatened by another man in his home, but not Tristan. While he waited for the water to heat up in the kettle, he leaned back, hands braced on the lip of the counter on either side of his hips.

"Are you all right with me marrying your mother? I didn't have a chance to meet you before I proposed. Lizzy and I both got a little eager. Now she's afraid we rushed things and that we should have talked to you kids first." Clayton seemed to be waiting for some type of reaction.

Tristan crossed his arms and met Clayton stare for stare. "My mother is a grown woman who is allowed to make her own choices. So long as you don't treat her like my father did, we shouldn't have a problem."

"Fair enough. That's something I can promise you." A dark look lingered on Clayton's face, and he changed whatever he'd been about to say. "I love Lizzy. Madly," he added, the pain in his eyes fading, replaced by a soft warmth.

"Good." It was all Tristan could get out. His throat tightened, and he had trouble swallowing. If his mother was happy, then he was happy.

"I know my daughter is a little younger than you, but I

hope you don't mind spending some time with her. She's hesitant about making friends, which is my fault. I moved her much too often. I think someone like you, as an older brother, could really help her gain some confidence to explore life. I'm sure you have a lot you want to do while you're home for Christmas, but it would mean a lot if you could include Kat." Clayton sipped his coffee again.

"I—" Before he could reply, his mother strode in, all smiles.

"Dear!" She walked over to where Clayton was sitting and brushed her lips over his before turning her face his way. "Tristan, you're up early."

"Mum." Tristan smiled.

"Did Clayton tell you? I've got a great idea for you and Kat to bond today. We need a new tree, and I thought you two could select one for us."

His mother's joy was impossible to resist, and he found himself nodding and murmuring, "Anything you want, Mum." As she embraced him, he noticed Clayton watching them, a smile half-hidden behind his coffee mug.

He thinks I'll be a good older brother to Kat... He has no idea what I really want to do to her.

A day alone with Kat. Even though he should've been running like hell in the opposite direction for both their sakes, he couldn't say no. The question was, how upset she was going to be when she found out? It was a pity he couldn't kiss away any protests. Kissing was off-limits. No matter how much he wanted to pin her against the wall and remind her just how hot a single kiss between them could be.

◈

"CHRISTMAS TREE SHOPPING?" KAT GLARED AT HER DAD. "No way. I'm not doing that."

Her father stood in her bedroom doorway, his mouth formed a hard line. It unsettled her. She didn't like to upset her father.

"What?" she snapped.

Her father sighed. "What's the matter, honey? Tristan is happy to go with you."

And that was the problem. *Tristan.*

"You know he's a womanizing playboy, right? You're okay with me being around him?" she asked, testing her father's reaction. It was stupid of her to want him to tell her to steer clear of Tristan. It wouldn't have erased that irresistible urge to be with him, but it would have helped buoy her attempts to deny his charm. Instead of warning her off, her dad was practically shoving her into Tristan's arms.

Her father just laughed. "Lizzy warned me. He's a bit wild, and I know he's ended up in the papers over some scandals, but Lizzy says he's a good kid, and the photos damage his father more than him. He's been good so far, and I'm not worried about you, honey. You're not his type."

Kat winced. *Ouch. Cut to the bone by my own father.*

"Kat, please. He's going to be family soon. It would make Lizzy happy, and what makes her happy makes *me* happy. Would you do it for me?" Her father patted her shoulder in encouragement.

She stared at him in complete shock. He'd never asked her to do anything before, not like this. Did it really matter to him that she spent time with Tristan?

"Okay." She sighed.

And that was how, two hours later, she was rushing to keep up with Tristan's long strides as he headed across the intersection, past waiting cars, toward the massive edifice of Harrods department store. The windows lining the sidewalks were wreathed with garlands wound with red silk ribbons and glittering Christmas lights, which accented the window displays. Scenes full of Santas and elves carrying presents to full-sized sleighs filled the massive windows. Others depicted Christmas through the ages, with various mannequins in elaborate costumes around fireplaces from the late Victorian era through the modern day. Each window was a stunning display of color, lights, and decorations.

"Wow." Harrods at Christmas was incredible.

So much color, so much life. Kat had never cared for Christmas. It had always felt like just another day to her, but seeing this and being with Tristan, it felt different. *Wonderful.* Everything around her seemed to glow, and it wasn't just the lights glinting from the windows. It was the way Tristan was looking at her, smiling, their hands close enough to touch. God, she wanted that so much it hurt, and right now it felt possible to be with him.

They were just two people out Christmas shopping, merging with other Londoners on the crowded sidewalks. She could pretend they were a couple, and that there wasn't anything forbidden about them being together. Her lips parted as she took a deep breath, embracing the moment. She must have looked silly because Tristan chuckled and reached for her hand. "You'll get used to the crowds. Come on."

Kat only hesitated a moment, enjoying the experience of putting her hand in his and the sense of connection that came when he curled his fingers around hers. For a brief moment she could slip into the universe that circled this sexy, charming man and believe that she belonged there.

He gave her hand a little squeeze when she didn't pull free of his hold. It was just the two of them, all alone, no parents. There were no secrets, no social or familial barriers keeping them apart now. Surely one day of hand-holding wouldn't be a risk. In the holiday rush no one would notice the two of them on a quick errand. She dodged the flurry of shoppers and icy water splashing from the street as taxicabs and tour buses rumbled past them.

Tristan picked a store door at random and led her inside. The scent of cinnamon and nutmeg surrounded her, the aromas carrying her back to snowy memories of building forts and making cocoa with her dad when they'd lived in Michigan for a year.

Color was everywhere; stacks of brightly decorated boxes, toys, and chocolates were on display. Anything and everything anyone could want filled the open shopping areas. It was overwhelming.

"Do you know where the trees are?" she asked Tristan as she followed him, her hand still curled in his, the grip warm through their gloved hands. They dodged babies in strollers and small children who were being wrangled by their frazzled mothers with full shopping baskets.

"This way," he said, indicating where to go. After they'd meandered through several huge departments, Tristan tugged her to a stop in front of a massive display of trees. "I hope you weren't expecting a live one." Tristan laughed and released her hand.

Kat instantly felt the loss of his touch, but she forced herself to focus on the trees. "Artificial is better," she said. "I can't stand to use a real one, not after reading the Hans Christian Andersen story *The Fir Tree*."

His lips thinned into a grimace. "Agreed. That man had a way of traumatizing little children. Between that, the Little Mermaid, and the matchstick girl story..." He trailed off with a theatrical shudder that had her suppressing a giggle.

"So we agree on artificial." Kat walked the length of the tree displays, studying each option: flashing lights, no lights, and snow-frosted trees. "Dad and I usually had a small tree we unpacked each year. I'm not used to picking something so big and..."

Permanent. Dad was getting married. This would be the family Christmas tree for years to come. The tree that she'd share with Tristan and his mother every year for the rest of... forever. How in the hell was she going to live the rest of her life with him after everything they'd done? Just play stepsiblings and ignore the fact that he'd taken her virginity and showed her how wonderful sex could be? Her throat constricted, and she battled the dueling emotions of panic and sadness.

Hands gripped her shoulder, stilling her in place so she couldn't continue her restless pacing.

"It's only a tree," Tristan reminded her. "Let's select one without lights, and we'll have the pleasure of decorating it ourselves. We'll get a tall one so it can be seen through the front windows."

He stood so close behind her that Kat had to fight the urge to lean back into him. If only she could give in to everything she was feeling in that moment, the need to connect to him, to cling to him when her life seemed to be spinning wildly out of control. His hands rubbed her coat-covered arms before he leaned over and pointed at one of the trees. It was a seven-foot beauty.

"That one?" she whispered, her breath suddenly quick. His cheek touched hers, and her whole body flushed with heat and awareness.

"That one," he murmured. Before she could react, he brushed his lips against her temple and left her side to wave over a store clerk. Little sparks of heat still burned where he'd kissed her, teasing her with that flame of desire she couldn't extinguish.

Kat stayed put, watching as Tristan gestured to the tree and handed the clerk a slim black credit card. It took her a few deep breaths to calm herself. If little innocent kisses like that were going to send her into a lust overdrive, she was going to have serious problems.

Tristan was impossible to ignore. Every look, touch, caress, or kiss was going to wreak havoc on her if she didn't find a way to turn her reactions off. She wasn't a robot; she couldn't ignore how he made her feel or how her body reacted.

I'm so screwed...

A few minutes later the clerk returned with his card and a receipt. Tristan waved the receipt in the air, grinning as he walked over to her.

"It should be delivered first thing tomorrow. We have plenty of lights and ornaments from last year."

"That's good. We can decorate it tomorrow night. I don't know how we would've gotten that tree back home by ourselves," she said and flinched.

Lizzy's town house was becoming home. It was all so strange...to know that her life was drastically changing. Kat and her father would be living in England. She'd been so busy acting like a petulant child and worrying about avoiding Tristan that she hadn't even thought to ask her dad about what this marriage meant long-term. Tristan would be in her life *forever*. She couldn't afford to mess things up for her dad by getting involved with her stepbrother.

God, I'm so selfish. The thought was so punishing, Kat actually winced.

"What's the matter?" Tristan cupped her chin and tilted her head back.

She almost pulled away from him, but as always, his hands on her made it hard to think.

Around them, the sounds of children laughing and the Christmas music humming from hidden speakers ran rampant on her emotions, and she sniffled.

"It's nothing," she lied.

"Kat, please, talk to me." His voice was low, rough with emotion. "You know you can tell me anything."

God, the man was killing her with his tender concern. He was also right. Talking with him had always been easy. She'd shared so much of herself with him that she couldn't imagine holding back anything. Yet she fought now to do just that. The last thing she wanted was for him to discover what was in her heart.

He smoothed the pad of his thumb over her bottom lip, and that treacherous little ache to kiss him, *to be kissed...* burned inside her. Memories of other kisses, of other nights with him, flashed before her eyes, and the need for his mouth on hers was almost too much. She started to lean into him before she caught herself and stepped back.

Why do I have to be so afraid of loving him? She wanted to scream, to rage and curse, but she couldn't do any of that. All she could do was stare up at Tristan, feeling like she was bleeding on the inside.

"I really don't want to talk about it. Can we just go? Please?" If she had to talk about everything that was tearing her up, she'd never survive, not when he was staring down at her with such pity.

"Of course, darling." His intense gaze softened, and he took hold of her hand again.

Darling. Why did his calling her that sound so wonderfully intimate? Like they were true lovers, not two people dancing around each other to avoid making a huge mistake?

They wandered through the department store, admiring decorations, presents, and window displays.

As they entered a different part of the store, Tristan halted, and Kat bumped into him from behind.

"What—" she stammered as she peered around his tall body, then gasped.

Ahead of them, filling the room, were three massive

display sets. To the left, a young woman stood at the window of a vine-covered tower, her braid of corn silk–colored hair reaching to the ground. A young man in slightly medieval garb held fast to the vines, as though ready to climb.

A female photographer was snapping photos furiously and suggesting poses.

The other display had a woman in a flowing blue ball gown descending a set of gray stone steps. A prince stood on the top step, reaching for her. Between them lay a single glass slipper, shimmering and iridescent.

By the time Kat's gaze swept to the third set, she realized what she was looking at. Fairy tale displays with live actors. Rapunzel, Cinderella, and the last... An empty glass coffin on a bed of flowers in a wooded glen, covered partly in snow. White birch trees sheltered the area, and snow falling from above created a fanciful dusting over the whole scene.

Snow White.

"Oh, you're perfect!" someone gasped.

Startled, Kat clenched a hand around Tristan's arm.

A petite young woman with spiky black hair and a face with delicate features beamed at her and Tristan. She brandished an expensive-looking camera.

"Perfect for what?" Tristan asked, one brow arching as he shot that imperious *"I'll be an earl someday"* look at the photographer.

"My photo shoot. I'm Jillian, by the way. The other photographers have found their couples, but I haven't found mine yet. Until I saw you two. Natural chemistry. You *have* to come with me." She grabbed Kat's free hand and dragged her toward a small changing room about ten feet away from the Snow White set.

"You're a size medium?" the photographer asked Kat, who, stunned by everything, just managed a tiny nod.

"Wonderful." The photographer dashed over to a costume

rack, handed her a red velvet gown, and shoved her toward a fitting room.

"And you, Prince!" the woman snapped at Tristan, who blinked, glanced at Kat, then, with an amused grin, shrugged and followed the photographer to another fitting room beside Kat's.

"What exactly will be done with these shots?" Tristan asked. "Nothing public?"

Jillian had her back to him while she rummaged around in her camera bag. "It's a charity contest, I'm using the shots to build my portfolio."

Kat glanced at Tristan who didn't seem fully convinced, but if they were only going in a portfolio that didn't sound too bad.

"Let's do it, Tristan. It could be fun." She grinned at him.

With a heavy sigh, he fixed her with an imperious look. "I'll only do this for you." He then scowled at the costume the photographer had handed him and stalked into a dressing room.

She took her costume into a second fitting room, studying the complex gown. "What the—" Kat bit off a curse as she tried to figure out how to unlace the back.

"You all right in there?" Tristan's voice came from somewhere beside her.

"Yeah...trying to figure out how to get into this thing." She continued to examine the skirt.

"I thought you liked these sort of gowns." Tristan's voice was a little muffled. "I distinctly recall you telling me in bed the other night that you wished women could wear gowns like that instead of some of the dresses they wear today."

It always shocked her how much he really listened to her.

"These gowns are great in theory, but I've never had to put on petticoats before."

His low, rough chuckle sent delicious shivers through her. "I'd be more than happy to come over and help you—"

"No peeking, Prince!" Jillian's voice cut into their conversation. A blush heated Kat's face when she realized that the photographer had heard the entire exchange.

Stripping out of her jeans and sweater, Kat pulled on the underskirt and petticoats. When she dropped the skirt over the underskirts, it created a wide shape around her hips and made her waist look tiny. The bodice was creamy white silk embroidered with flowers, and red velvet sleeves puffed at the shoulders. In a few minutes she'd transformed from Kat into Snow White.

"You ready to be laced up?" Jillian's voice was slightly muffled on the other side of the changing room door.

"Yes." She reached for the door handle and, the second it was open an inch, the photographer burst inside like a force of nature and made quick work of the laces.

"Shoes..." Jillian stared at Kat's feet for a few seconds, then she went to a small portable rack, selected a pair of gold brocade slippers, and handed them to Kat.

"Try these."

Dropping the slippers to the floor, Kat lifted her skirts and slipped into them. They fit perfectly. Just like the dress.

"Excellent!" The photographer clapped her hands together. "Let's get you settled, and I'll fetch your prince."

Kat curled her fingers in her skirts and followed the photographer to the snowy display area. The glass coffin was shallow and perched on an authentic-looking wooden glen dusted with snow. It was so realistic that it was easy to forget this was only a set.

"Now, just lie down in the glass coffin and take this." The photographer handed her a shiny red apple.

With the fruit in one hand and her skirts in the other, Kat ascended the half-hidden steps to reach the coffin. She climbed in, lay down on the white pillows inside, and rearranged her skirts.

"Take a bite of the apple," the photographer called out.

Kat bit into the apple, chewing on the crisp fruit, and then stared up at the ceiling. A huge net of fake snow was straight over her head.

"Shut your eyes and let one hand drop to your side, barely clutching the apple."

The woman made a graceful gesture with her arm, and Kat mimicked it.

"Perfect. Now close your eyes."

Breathing in slowly, she felt the corset tighten around her breasts. Kat shut her eyes, letting the scene sweep her away in her mind.

Here and here alone she could have Tristan.

Only in a fairy tale.

$$\approx \quad 8 \quad \approx$$

"She's ready." The little pixie of a photographer latched onto Tristan's arm and dragged him out of the dressing room.

They walked a few steps away from the changing area and Tristan glanced at the other two sets, committing every detail to memory. He wanted to remember this moment with Kat forever.

"May I have copies of the photos when they're ready?" He didn't want the rest of the world to see, but he certainly wanted copies for himself.

The photographer glanced down at the camera, then looked up at him.

"Sure. I can send you copies after I've retouched them for my portfolio." She handed him a business card with her contact information on it. "Though," she added. "You could do with a bit of good publicity, Mr. Kingsley."

Tristan halted. "You are not to breathe a word of this to anyone. I don't want those photos to go public." He glanced around the large area. "Is this a closed set?" He didn't want a customer from the department store who might recognize him stumbling into this area.

She pressed a fingertip to her lips. "Yes, I'll shut the doors in a minute. It will be closed." She winked at him, then pointed at the set ahead of them. "Go wake her up, dear prince."

He looked in the direction she pointed and lost his breath. Cushioned on silk inside a shallow glass coffin, Kat lay as if asleep. Her dark hair rippled in wild waves over the pillow and mingled with the light snow that had started to fall from the rafters above. A crimson apple lay at the tips of her fingers, and a pearly light illuminated her pale, perfect skin. It was startling and stunning in contrast to the red gown she wore.

The hustle and bustle of the holiday shoppers faded away. He was completely lost in this strange, surreal experience. Just him, alone with Kat, *his* Snow White.

"She looks like a dream... What do I do?" he whispered, half to himself and half to the photographer. For the first time in his life, the sight of a woman had halted in him his tracks.

The photographer nudged him gently in the back. "I want you to walk up behind the coffin, kneel down, and kiss her. Do it slowly so I can shoot various angles and poses as you move. I'll tell you when to stop."

Another nudge, this one much firmer, forced him to stumble forward a step. The knee-high buckskin boots made his steps almost silent as he approached the snow-covered glen.

Mirror, mirror on the wall... His lips twitched. *I've found the fairest of them all.*

The faux snowfall thickened, coating his hair and his clothes as he climbed up the rocky steps leading to the grassy area of the glen behind the coffin. Kat's breathing was so faint he could barely see the swell of her breasts against the bodice. Kneeling beside the glass structure that held her, he touched the clear edge of the coffin. She looked so delicate and vulnerable, but he knew how strong she could be, too.

Here, now, she's mine. I don't have to share her with anyone. He needed this moment, just the two of them; he needed her. It was a scary thing to realize, but there was no point in denying it any longer.

Hesitating for only a heartbeat, he leaned over Kat and kissed her. Her mouth trembled against his as he startled her as though waking her from a dream. Electric tingles of arousal and awareness sparked through him. Taunting, torturing.

I shall never get enough of her. He stroked his tongue along the seam of her mouth, and she parted her lips with a little exhalation of surprise. Tristan had always been one to enjoy kissing, but with Kat, it was something entirely different than it had been with any other woman. It was as necessary as breathing.

He didn't want to think about what would happen when this was over, when they had to return to the town house as stepsiblings and nothing more. As he kissed her, he let go of the world around them. The only thing left was her, and despite the snowflakes landing on their skin, he only felt her. Her mouth, her essence, the feel of his heart reaching out to hers. One of her slender hands cupped his jaw, gently keeping him close as their mouths mated.

She was the first to break the kiss, but only to gasp. Tristan opened his eyes, and for a long second they stared at each other. A hint of tears shimmered in her eyes, and he felt his own body quake and shudder with a rush of unexpected feelings. He tried to smile, but everything in him felt...raw.

With a great struggle to regain his wits, he attempted to

put some levity into the moment, lest the strange flood of emotions carry him off. "Better than butterflies?" he whispered.

Her hand, still on his jaw, caressed his skin, as Kat nodded. "Better than stained glass?"

He blinked and glanced away, heat suffusing his face. He still couldn't believe he'd told her that. He'd never told that to *anyone* before because it made him look weak. It was bloody frightening, letting someone see that deep into his soul.

"I hate that we can't..." He sighed and kissed her again, stealing another all-too-fleeting moment of bliss. Why couldn't they stay like this forever?

"Me, too."

He touched his forehead to hers and closed his eyes again, savoring this brief time to just be with her.

"That's perfect!" The photographer's shout cut through their secret fairy-tale world of half-bitten apples, glass coffins, and falling snow.

It had been perfect. Too bad it wasn't real. And he hated knowing it wasn't.

Together they turned to look at Jillian, who was grinning.

"You're going to love these shots!" she said, proudly parading about near the small camera tool table as she set her camera down.

Finally Tristan got to his feet and reached for Kat, lifting her above the edge of the coffin. She felt so good in his arms that he couldn't resist pulling her against his chest for a brief moment before setting her down.

Snow billowed out around her feet when her skirts swished as she took a few steps toward the edge of the set. He rushed after her, catching her arm to support her down the steps.

"Thank you," she murmured, leaning closer than necessary and gripping his arm.

"Anything for you," he said. And he meant every word.

A pink blush stained her cheeks and she pulled free, as though she'd realized she'd let herself slip in her intent to keep distance between them. They walked over to the table where the photographer was standing.

Tristan crossed his arms and faced the photographer, while Kat rushed off to the changing room.

"These won't be shared with the paparazzi, correct?" He wanted to make doubly sure that these photos wouldn't surface. "What about whoever judges the photos? I don't want them selling them to the press."

Jillian shook her head. "No, that can't happen. The photos are my intellectual property. If they were leaked, I'd be able to sue for damages. I won't let them get leaked. I promise."

"Good." He stared at the photographer a second longer before he we went to change back into his clothes.

As he stripped out of the doublet, his mind kept replaying the kiss. How soft Kat's lips were, how her little tongue played with his, and the way she'd stroked his jaw. Tender and trembling with excitement. Every time he kissed her felt like the first time. Something he hadn't thought possible after all the women he'd kissed in the past. It was as though Kat had been made just for him, a dream come true. It sounded like a foolish fantasy of a boy, but he didn't care. She made him feel...wonderful. There was no jaded bitterness from life when he was with her. Everything seemed possible.

Jillian was waiting for him when he emerged from the dressing room. "I owe you both. These photos will be phenomenal. The other two artists found their couples right away, but I hadn't seen anyone I liked with natural chemistry. How long have you been together?" Jillian smiled and started packing up her camera gear.

"Oh, we're not—" Kat began at the same time Tristan said, "We aren't—"

Jillian's eyes darted between them, and she winked. "One of those hush-hush, will-they- or-won't-they situations, huh? I get it. My boyfriend and I were like that when we both started working at the same studio. Secret shagging is so hot, am I right?"

Kat gaped at Jillian, but Tristan had to cough to hide a laugh. The woman was absolutely right about secret sex. Normally he hated photographers because they ruined his life and violated his privacy, but perhaps this Jillian wasn't so bad.

"Well, I've got to dash. Got a shoot at the National Portrait Gallery in half an hour. I'll send you the proofs." She zipped up the last of her bags and left with another little wink and a smile at them.

They were alone with the massive fairy-tale set, and Tristan wanted to drag Kat back to the glass coffin and wake her up with another kiss.

"Well...uh..." He shoved his hands into his trouser pockets, at a loss for words.

"I guess we should go back to the town house." Kat grabbed her coat and pulled it on, her kissable mouth turned down in a little frown.

He didn't like to see her that way. "Kat—" Tristan had only just gotten that out before someone called his name.

"Tristan Kingsley?"

"Yes?" Tristan spun in the direction of the voice that'd called out to him.

A camera flashed and the world turned white. A few seconds later, he blinked owlishly to get rid of the large white dots in his field of vision. When he could see again, he nearly stumbled back a step at the sight of three photographers, each gripping a camera and staring at him with a hungry expression.

"It's him!" one of them whispered loudly. They all raised their cameras again.

Paparazzi. Where the bloody hell was security? Probably swamped with shoppers at the cashiers and not watching the upper floors.

"Who's the lady with you, Mr. Kingsley?" another of the paparazzi demanded.

Shoving Kat behind him, he waved a hand in their direction. "No pictures," he growled, then moved fast. Shielding Kat with one arm around her shoulders, he whispered into her ear, "Run! This way!" They bolted through the store, dodging racks of clothes and piles of beautifully wrapped present displays.

"Mr. Kingsley!" The shouts echoed from behind them, and Tristan knew they needed to find a place to lie low for a while

"Tristan, why won't they leave us alone?" Kat glanced up at him, her beautiful gray eyes wide and tinged with shock.

"I'm sorry. We'll find a way to lose them." He led her around a woman whose children were admiring a case of new video games. About ten feet away, an employee exited a storage closet.

Brilliant! Tugging Kat toward it, he opened the door and shoved her inside. She squealed in surprise, and he dove in after her. Then he closed the door and waited.

"Trist—"

He clamped a hand over her mouth. Just outside he could hear the paparazzi talking to one another.

"He's here somewhere. I saw him go this way," a man said.

"Who was he with? Bit of a mouse compared to his usual standards. Wonder what happened with Brianna Wolverton."

Tristan silently snarled. Kat was fucking beautiful, and here she was, eyes brimming with tears. He dropped his hand from her mouth and stared at her lips.

"Don't listen to a word they say," he breathed, just loudly enough for her to hear. "You're intoxicating." He edged closer, that predatory need to capture her and make her his beginning to whisper in his veins with a delicious thrill.

"I am?" Kat licked her lips and tilted her head back, retreating until her back hit the wall.

Nowhere to run. One corner of his mouth kicked up in a half-grin.

"Yes. More than anyone I've ever met." He placed one hand on the wall beside her head and his other on the flare of her full, womanly hip. "So much," he paused and slowly lowered his head, "that I can't go another minute without kissing you." He brought his lips to hers in a kiss that was stolen and wicked, with a hint of roughness.

Outside, the paparazzi would be circling, hoping to find them, but for now, he could take his time with her. She couldn't escape unless she wanted to end up on the front page of the tabloids.

With a little moan against his lips, Kat clutched the lapels of his coat and clung to him, kissing him back. Her touch made him want to go all the way, take her here in a bloody broom closet. He needed to keep himself in check. Snatching her wrists, he pinned them on either side of her head and used his whole body to trap her against the wall. Images from earlier assaulted him, driving him mad with desire. He wanted his Snow White, to taste the fruit of an apple upon her lips.

Full lips, eyelashes dusted with snow. Alabaster white skin and the tempting gleam of an apple, its juices coating her tongue as she kissed him back.

He'd experienced something beyond roleplay, and for a few brief moments, they had lived a fairy tale together. Tristan didn't want her to escape, not this woman whose kiss resonated with him on such a deep level.

Nibbling at her lips, he enticed her to open her mouth further, allowing him to delve inside. After all the wild and sexy women he'd been with, this one, this innocent but innately sensual woman, was going to undo him.

He released her hands so he could cup her arse and clench it hard, earning a responding gasp and rock of her pelvis toward his.

"That's it, darling, show me your dark side," he whispered against her lips.

"Please, Tristan," she begged, and the little minx brazenly cupped his cock through his trousers.

He cursed in torture and pleasure at her stroking touch. "Please what?" he asked, moving his mouth to her neck, sucking and nipping, leaving little love bites against her skin. A wild need to mark her had turned him almost feral. He'd always loved a rough tumble in the sheets, but this was...so much more. Purely primal.

"Please fu—"

A sharp rattle of a doorknob cut through the dense fog of his lust, and a shaft of bright light burst between him and Kat.

"What the... You shouldn't be in here!" An angry male store clerk in his red Harrods shirt glared at them. A shiny red name tag proclaimed that his name was "Glenn."

Tristan recovered more quickly than Kat, and he laced his fingers through hers, dragging her past the scowling store clerk. "Pardon us, *Glenn*."

They darted through the store and back onto the street without encountering any more paparazzi. Relieved, Tristan hailed a cab and ushered Kat inside. "Kew Gardens, please," he told the driver.

"Very good, sir." The driver set his fare machine and pulled out into traffic.

Tristan slid an arm around Kat's shoulders and tugged her close so that their hips and legs touched. She was blushing and biting her lip to keep from giggling. It was one of his favorite expressions of hers, and he loved knowing he'd put it there. This delighted look of near laughter was almost as perfect as one of her smiles. For once she wasn't worrying about the consequences of being with him. She was the way she should be: a happy woman.

"Being with you is a bit of a whirlwind, isn't it?" she asked.

He beamed. "Life isn't worth living unless you fill every second with adventure."

"Making out in a Harrods storage closet was certainly an adventure." She laughed.

"It was, wasn't it? And kissing Snow White. I'll cross that off my fantasy bucket list." He leaned over to press a kiss to her temple, and she placed her head in the crook of his shoulder, sighing in contentment.

"Tristan," she murmured, her eyes darkening with shadows as she put one hand on his lower stomach, rubbing him slowly, soothing, as she cuddled closer. "We have to figure out what we're going to do."

Her whispered words gave him a glimmer of hope. It was the first time she seemed to be considering their being together as inevitable.

I'll fight to have you, Kat. Fight you, our parents, the world. You belong to me.

"We'll talk tonight. I don't want to ruin today. Not when we're headed to the best part."

"And what's that?" Kat asked.

Tristan tightened his arm around her shoulders, loving the feel of her body so close to his.

"Kew Gardens. They happen to have a special exhibit of butterflies."

Her eyes widened, revealing those mercury gray pools he could easily lose himself in.

"Butterflies?" she whispered.

He nodded. "Once upon a time, you told me you loved them. What kind of gentleman would I be if I didn't give you your heart's desire?"

❅   *9*   ❅

"I want you to have everything you love, Kat," Tristan said softly.

What if all I want is you?

She couldn't tell him that, and he could never know how deep her feelings for him ran. He could break her heart, their parents could split up and get hurt...too much was at risk. What would he do if he learned she was falling in love with him?

"I just want to have fun with you today." With a few rapid blinks of her eyes to clear the newly forming tears, she took a deep breath and sat back, determined to enjoy the half-hour ride to Kew Gardens.

After the taxi had dropped them off, she and Tristan walked down the wide, open path toward the glass edifice in the distance. Evergreen trees were dusted with snow and sunlight illuminated the ice beneath their feet, making it shimmer and sparkle like crushed diamonds.

"Come on, you have to see this," Tristan said before trotting toward a magnificent tree that stood at the northern end of the Broad Walk.

Covered in snow, an old, thick-trunked tree spread its branches out in a wild fan.

"This is an oriental plane tree. They call it the 'Old Lion.' It was planted around 1762." Tristan pressed a palm to the bark and looked her way. The boyish charm he wielded to devastating perfection tugged at her heart.

Unable to resist, she walked over to join him, placing her hand next to his, feeling the rough scrape of the cold bark. "How do you know all of this?" she asked.

He glanced away, a hint of sadness in his eyes. "My mother used to bring me here as a child. She loves flowers, and whenever she was sad or hurting, we came here to escape our lives for a few hours."

The picture he painted was a melancholy one. A strained, unhappy woman and her tiny son, wandering among the gardens, happy to find some measure of peace. Not unlike the way her father used to sit on the edge of her bed and read her stories of Verne's metal ships beneath the sea, of mighty squid and hot-air balloons uplifted to the skies to begin grand adventures.

She and Tristan had more in common than she'd realized. They'd both been hurt by one parent and were desperate to protect their other parent from the pain of the world. It wasn't a duty a child was meant to have, but when you loved someone, you did what was necessary to protect them. In this one way they were the same. *It's why we understand each other on a deeper level.*

"The entrance is this way." He covered her hand with his, calling Kat out of her thoughts.

As she followed him toward the building, she glanced back at the Old Lion tree, wondering if it would last another two hundred and fifty years. Some things could stand the test of time.

The interior of Kew Gardens was bright and rich with

color. Perfumed scents from a multitude of flowers filled the air. Winter's frost had no power inside this gigantic hothouse. Archways were covered in the purple blooms of wisteria which swung hypnotically in the slight breeze of the heated air. She and Tristan meandered down the path, admiring flowers as they went until they arrived at another room sealed by sliding doors. On the other side, a garden attendant monitored people coming and going from the next area of the conservatory.

"He's checking for butterflies," Tristan whispered in her ear. "They can cling to your clothes and you might not notice."

Following him, she reached for his hand, and he clasped her fingers warmly in his. Maybe they were damned, but at least they could be damned together. There was time enough to face the world when they got back to the town house.

As they passed through the sliding doors and into the butterfly garden, Kat gasped.

It was an eternal spring. Butterflies were everywhere. Pots full of nectar were nestled in all the nooks and crannies by the plants, and a hundred different species of butterflies were seamlessly floating about on the air. A large black butterfly with blue dots on its wings landed on Tristan's shoulder blade. He couldn't see it, and Kat laughed.

He looked down at her. "What?"

"You have a passenger catching a free ride on your right shoulder."

"Little bugger." Tristan chuckled and tried to crane his neck so he could see the butterfly.

It fanned its wings down flat as though settling in for the ride, which displayed the striking colors and patterns on its wings. It was alluring and seductive, and Kat couldn't resist reaching for it. Rather than flutter off, it moved onto her finger, its little antennae swiveling as it studied her. It touched her skin with its little butterfly tongue, searching for nectar.

"Hello," Kat whispered, marveling at the little insect.

Butterflies were so fragile, yet against all odds they survived, through storms, through frost, through almost anything except the extinction of their habitats. Her eyes burned with tears as she thought about the world losing butterflies one by one. They seemed such a small, insignificant part of the universe, but to Kat they were no less important than any other creature.

"Don't do that, darling," Tristan murmured and tipped her chin up so he could see her eyes.

"Do what?" she sniffed and attempted to smile.

"Cry. I never want to see you cry." He stroked a fingertip over her lips and chuckled.

"What?"

"Your little friend landed on your head. I think he winked at me. Do butterflies wink? If so, they are certainly the cheekiest little fellows..."

She knew Tristan was teasing her, but it made her laugh and kept the tears at bay.

"Your mom really brought you here as a child?" She still held his hand, and his fingers tightened around hers.

The blue-green of his eyes made her think of the waving colors of a kelp forest, just when sunlight cut through the gloom and illuminated the sea of green strands as they rippled through the deep water.

She and her father had lived in Monterey Bay only a year, but he'd taken her to the aquarium several times. It was there that she'd glimpsed sea otters frolicking about in the kelp forests. It had been peaceful and strangely enchanting to watch. Kat could have stood there forever, with her hands pressed to the tall glass of the underwater room, watching the kelp and the otters.

"It's hard for someone in my mother's place. She is the daughter of a peer, and she was expected to marry equal to or above her station. I think, when my father proposed, she was too young to realize that she didn't have to say yes. But there's so much pressure in this life to do what is expected of us. Her parents were little different than my father when it came to what they believed their daughter should do. Rather than give herself time to find true love, she let herself believe love would come in time with my father. That mistake cost her too much." The solemnity in his eyes made Kat's heart ache.

"Is that what's expected of you? To marry someone like..." She swallowed hard, trying not to think about him being with another woman, marrying someone else.

He didn't immediately answer her. Instead, he walked away a few feet and reached out to tap the petals of a large orange flower where a butterfly was settled. Half of the insect's wings were transparent.

"What kind is this one?" Tristan pointed at the butterfly. He was able to slide his finger underneath it, and the insect let him lift it up so Kat could see.

She smiled, a little sad. "A glasswing butterfly. It's from Central America and very rare. The tissue on its wings is so thin it's actually see-through."

"Magnificent," Tristan whispered, then he finally looked at her. "You see things in the world, small, wondrous things, and you do everything you can to learn about them. You have a passion for knowledge, and a gift for seeing endless wonder in things I so often take for granted." The smile upon his lips was carved from lines of grief rather than joy.

Kat's heart stuttered in her chest, and she raised her chin, trying to draw strength from deep inside as she replied, "Do you know what I like about you Tristan? You're not afraid to live."

For several moments they watched the butterflies twist and dance around them before Kat repeated her original question, but she feared she knew the answer.

"You have to marry someone like Brianna Wolverton, don't you?"

The heavy sigh that escaped his lips was a tomb being sealed upon her last hopes.

"It is what's expected of me. Whoever I marry will need to be capable of handling the pressures of society, politics, and managing the estate alongside me. Most women in my social circles have been raised since birth to handle this. I would be a fool if I said I didn't need to look at it rationally, no matter what I might wish otherwise." The finality in his tone told her that he didn't want to talk about it anymore. As sick as she felt in that moment, with her chest splitting open with pain, she didn't want to talk about it, either.

"Why did your mother bring you here and not somewhere else?"

"My father said and did many things that hurt my mother. I was only a lad, but I knew she needed peace and quiet so she could...recover. There was something about the flowers that soothed her."

A pit dropped into Kat's stomach. "He didn't hurt her... physically, I mean. Did he?"

Tristan captured a lock of her hair and spooled it around one finger, studying the strands as though they held the secrets of the universe.

"No. But some words hurt as much or more than physical blows. He made it clear that she was a disappointment, that she wasn't loved. Words like that can be devastating."

The way he said it made her wonder if he'd been a victim of his father's vicious words, as well. He seemed to have too much familiarity with that sort of pain.

Kat moved cautiously toward Tristan, checking to make

sure no little winged passengers were between them. Then she wrapped her arms around him in a fierce embrace. She held on as though she'd lose him at any minute. She let every warm, soft feeling and healing thought pour out of her into him. When his arms wound around her, just as strong, she nuzzled his chest, breathing in the scent she'd come to recognize as his clean aftershave, with a hint of pine and mint, and the warm, dark scent of man.

"What are you doing to me, Kat?" Tristan's voice was low and a little rough, and his arms were tight around her body as though he were afraid to let her go. "I can't see my future without you in it and I know I can't keep you, not forever, but I want to. If you want me, I would give everything I am to be with you. Do you understand? *Everything*." His eyes glowed with tenderness, passion, and something so deep and soft it shook her to the core. It couldn't be love—he didn't love her—but he was gazing at her like that and it... She gave herself a little shake, trying to think.

"Me? What about you?" she murmured. "I didn't want to like you this much. I didn't want to—" Unable to finish where that terrifying thought might be headed, she gently pushed away from him and wiped at her eyes. With a few shaky steps, she put space between them and pretended to study the butterflies wafting about the air before they landed on flowers.

It gave her the chance to think without losing herself in the comfort of his arms. One of them had to be reasonable enough to see that this couldn't go on between them. It wasn't simply because their parents were getting married. It was painfully clear that Tristan's path in life would take him far away from her.

I'm just a little nobody, an American, not a woman trained from birth to be the wife of a titled peer. I wouldn't know the first thing about being with him...not in the way I'd want to be.

"You're right. We have to decide what we're going to do," Tristan said.

When she turned to look at him, she nearly jumped. He was close again, right behind her, hunger and hope in his heated gaze. She placed a hand on his chest. "I need a little time."

His shoulders sagged, and he nodded, his brows knitting together and his lips wilting from the hopeful smile. Tristan clenched his fists and stared at a passing butterfly as though it could cure him of his lust.

"Maybe we should go home," she suggested.

"Maybe we should," he echoed. There was a hollowness to his tone that created a black, aching hole in her chest.

They left the gardens and crossed the snow-covered grounds again, silence settling between them like thick London fog. With each step, her heart turned inside out. Each splinter of pain tore into her until she couldn't breathe.

Tristan stared out the window as the cab he'd hailed pulled away from the curb. The distance between them was so wide that Kat wanted to crawl across the seat and cuddle up next to him. She wanted to be with him now, wanted to be in his arms and in his bed, but the cost to his future was too high.

The ride back to the town house seemed too long, and yet not long enough. Her mind had gone over a hundred options of how to make things work with Tristan, but there didn't seem to be any good solutions.

If we can just survive the holidays, we'll go back to school and probably not see each other. Then, after a few months, our desire for each other will have to cool, won't it?

As the cab pulled up in front of the town house, Lizzy appeared in the doorway. When they got out of the cab and walked up the steps, Kat noticed that Lizzy's eyes were red. She sniffed but held her chin up bravely. Clayton stood behind her, his expression a thunderous one Kat had never seen before.

"Mum?" Tristan moved straight to her, and Kat followed, as they all walked back into the house. "What's the matter?" he asked, glancing suspiciously at Kat's father, who held up his hands in surrender.

Lizzy sighed. "It's your father. You have to go to him tonight."

It took a moment for Lizzy's words to sink in. Tristan had to leave? *Tonight?*

"I promised I'd stay with you, Mum." Tristan didn't glance at Kat, but she felt his attention on her all the same.

She shook her head. "He wants you with him for the rest of the holidays."

"Mum, I don't have to—"

"You do." She sniffed. "I'm so sorry, Tristan. I had really hoped we could have this first Christmas together, all of us." Lizzy shared a sad little smile with Kat and reached for Clayton's hand, squeezing his fingers as they touched.

Kat understood that desire for physical comfort all too well. The thought of Tristan leaving made her want to cling to him.

For a long moment, Tristan didn't say a word, then he shoved his hands into his pockets and nodded as though making a decision.

"I suppose I ought to go, then." He let his mother kiss his cheek, then he ascended the stairs at a quick pace, leaving them all behind.

Leaving was a solution to their dilemma, but it left her feeling raw and hollow.

"I'm so sorry, Kat. Please excuse me." Lizzy covered her mouth with the back of her hand and blinked away tears.

"It's okay," Kat assured her, touching Lizzy's arm. Something about seeing Tristan's mother upset made her upset, too. "It would've been nice for all of us to be together for Christmas, but we'll have next year." She meant it. It was strange to have someone who cared about wanting to be around her, other than her dad, of course, but she liked being wanted.

Lizzy managed a smile, and Kat saw her dad frowning out of the corner of her eyes.

"I just wish Tristan's father wasn't such a..."

"Bully?" Kat replied without thinking. Heat rushed to her cheeks, and she glanced down. "Sorry. I shouldn't have said that."

"No," Lizzy straightened her shoulders. "You're right. The man is a bully. He heard about Clayton and me this morning, and it's made him furious."

"Tristan is an adult and can just say no, can't he?"

Lizzy clasped her hands, clenching her fingers tight. "It's not that simple. Tristan's father wields a lot of power, not just in politics, but in our lives. He pays for Tristan's schooling and his lifestyle. He's threatened to take all of that away if Tristan won't comply."

Kat's insides froze, and she shivered. "I can't imagine Tristan letting anyone force him to do something he doesn't want to do." She didn't want to know how Tristan was under his father's thumb, but she *needed* to know.

"It's complicated to explain, but part of it is that Tristan cares about everyone who works on the estate, especially Carter and his father, John Martin. Edward might fire John just to upset Tristan because it would force Carter to leave the estate as well, and he could deprive them of references to make it harder for them to find employment. It's medieval, but Edward is capable of much worse if he deems it necessary."

Someone would do that? How was it even possible that

someone would be so cruel? No wonder Tristan despised his father.

"Lizzy, sweetheart, why don't we go to the kitchen for some hot cocoa and tea?" Her father curled an arm around Lizzy's waist and kissed her forehead, the act intimate and loving. *He really does love her.* Kat swallowed past the lump in her throat. *Tristan kissed me like that only an hour ago...* The flood of warmth inside her chest at the memory was soon torn apart. He was leaving her.

"Do you like tea?" Lizzy asked her, holding out a hand. Kat took it. "If not, we've plenty of cocoa. I find your father's sweet tooth endearing."

Clayton chuckled. "There's nothing wrong with a man admitting he likes sweet things, daughter and future wife included." He winked at Kat.

"Dad, seriously." She started to laugh even though her heart still burned at the thought of Tristan leaving.

"Yes, Clayton, you charmer." Lizzy nudged Clayton in the ribs and shared a smile with Kat.

"Come along, ladies. Hot drinks await."

Kat glanced at the stairs as she headed toward the kitchen. There was no sign of Tristan. She hoped he'd say good-bye, even though she hated good-byes. For him, she'd go through the pain, if it meant seeing him once more.

She closed her eyes, embracing the image of them in the Kew Gardens, butterflies all around them, no secrets, no distance between them. The way his smile had made her feel like she was in a freefall. Frightening but also exhilarating.

There was no stopping it.

He was leaving, and it was too late to find a way to keep him there.

$$\text{❧}\quad\text{I O}\quad\text{❧}$$

Tristan's heart weighed a thousand pounds. It crushed his ribs as he hefted his travel bag over his shoulder and walked down the stairs to the town house's front door.

The last thing he wanted to do was leave, but he had to. *Father dearest* demanded it. Under other circumstances, he would have refused to go, no matter the threats his father might make, but he needed to put distance between himself and Kat. Seeing how hurt she was by this whole situation...

The pain in his own chest was bad enough; he couldn't imagine how Kat was feeling, after she'd almost cried in his arms earlier that day. She knew as well as he did that this thing between them, as wonderful as it could be, wouldn't last, no matter how much they wanted it to. Life would eventually pull them apart. Their paths were set in divergent lines, spearing away to distant futures that would never cross again, except in family situations with their parents. He hadn't wanted to face that reality, and until today he'd been rebellious enough to think he could go on just as he had been, being with Kat and avoiding any of the consequences. But that wouldn't last forever. He would eventually settle down with a woman of his father's choosing. It was a death sentence upon his happiness. Even though he couldn't be with Kat in the long run, he still wanted to be with her *now*.

Maybe time and distance were the solution. If he went to Pembroke and didn't return to his mother's town house, he wouldn't have to face her for some time. Their classes at Cambridge would likely never put them close to each other.

Maybe then I can destroy the beating heart in my chest with her name carved into it.

Taking the stairs quickly, he was at the door when someone called his name, stopping him.

"You were going to leave without saying good-bye?" Kat asked as she came out of the study.

Had she been waiting for him to pass by? The thought filled him with a traitorous sense of hope. Why was his mind so determined to find reasons to come back to her? No woman had ever been worth this torment.

He set his bag on the ground and tugged his long Burberry trench coat close about his body, slipping the buttons into their slits.

"I didn't think you'd want to." Why the comment came out so cold, he wasn't sure. Perhaps he could pretend he didn't care. It was a lie, but he wanted to believe it.

"Stop that!" she snapped, her gray eyes shining with tears. "You know I don't like good-byes." She stepped closer as she spoke, her eyes full of emotions he wished she'd surrender to.

All he wanted was to drag her into his arms and kiss her. Remind her that what existed between them was beyond ordinary. That he would put everything in his life at risk to have a future with her.

Even he had to admit that what lay between them was no longer pure lust. It was something far greater, far deeper. It scared the bloody hell out of him.

"Why are you so afraid of us being together?" he demanded in a gruff whisper

"'Why?'" She moved another precious step closer. "Because if I stop and think about what could happen, what will happen, it frightens me. I'm not what you need. And when you finally figure that out, it will be too late for me. I'll be so in love with you by then and..." She swallowed hard. "I'm afraid I'll never get over loving you and not being with you."

She thinks she's falling in love with me? His heart leaped into his throat, and he suddenly had trouble swallowing. The thought of her loving him sent a strange thrill deep through him, pouring into his blood and spreading like an inner fire. Right now she was his, and he wanted to be the only man she ever loved. And he wanted no other woman but her.

Tristan cupped her face, cursing the crystalline tears clinging to her sooty lashes. The sight of those tears knotted his stomach, and he forced himself to draw in a painful breath.

He was on a ragged edge of desperation, tethered to her, as if they were a pair of tiny boats in a mighty storm, but he felt that invisible rope between them fraying. He couldn't let go, not yet, even though he knew it was best for everyone if he did.

"Darling, please, you're killing me," he murmured and stole her mouth in a slow, sweet kiss that sent strange, but not unwelcome, tremors through him. A woman had never affected him like this, made him shake from just a kiss. He felt light-headed, giddy, and yet everything was tinged with the aching sadness of having to leave her.

We belong together... The realization hummed through him like the distant vibration of a thousand bees around a hive in the midst of summer. The sensation was comforting, yet it was all too fleeting. There were only a few minutes left for him to embrace her and kiss her. He poured every tender thought, every little, sweet thing she made him feel into this kiss.

Her lips trembled, and she curled her arms around his neck, pressing her body to his. Every time he held Kat in his arms, Tristan wanted it to last forever.

His cell phone buzzed in his pants pocket, and he separated himself from Kat with a muttered curse. His father's number flashed across the screen. The only person who could keep him from having Kat, the man who would destroy any chance of his ever being happy, all for his own selfish reasons.

Damn him! Even at a distance his father was determined to ruin the best thing that had ever happened to him.

"It's your father, isn't it?"

He pocketed the phone with a grim nod. "Yes. I'm delayed, and it's going to make him even angrier than usual." He headed for the front door.

Kat covered her lips with her fingertips as Tristan retrieved his bag from the floor and swung it over his shoulder. He gripped the door handle again and glanced her way, his heart beating wildly as he offered himself to her one last time.

"If you want me, you know how to reach me. All you need to do is say *yes* and I'll come to you. But I won't come back unless you want me." He couldn't be around her if he couldn't have her. He didn't have the inner strength to control himself. Until Kat was ready to fight for him as much as he wanted to fight for her, there wasn't any other choice but to leave. The moment she realized she was strong enough, he'd come running.

"But your mother..." Kat rushed over to the door, gripping his arm to stop him from leaving.

He shook his head. "If I'm to do as you wish and keep my distance, this is the only way. I'm sorry, Kat." Reaching up to twine one lock of her hair around his finger, one last touch before he left, he smiled, but it was a melancholy smile. "Have a Happy Christmas." The words were so rough and low, he wasn't sure if she heard him. But she bit her bottom lip and nodded, not saying anything.

The silence cut him apart, but he would never let her know how much.

He opened the door and walked to his car. He took the keys from the footman and put his bag in the trunk before chancing one look back at the town house.

Kat stood in the doorway, looking small and vulnerable in her jeans and thick sweater. She rubbed her arms and watched him silently. A light breeze played with her hair, tugging strands over her face, but she didn't move to brush them away.

Good-bye, sweet Kat.

Tristan opened the car door and slipped inside, gunned the engine to life, and sped away.

The streets were wet and dark, and the tires crunched as he hit small patches of icy snow. The drive would clear his head, and by the time he reached the Pembroke Estate he'd be ready to deal with his father.

A little under an hour later, he drove through the main gates of Pembroke and waved at the security guards in their little stone cottage just past the entrance. Ahead of him, the massive family home loomed out of the woods, the tan stones a dusty gold in the winter sun. He left the car in the drive by the main door and handed the keys to the waiting footman, who hurried to take the car to one of the garages. Tristan was barely inside before he saw Carter lounging in the doorway of the morning room.

"Lurking in doorways is a bad habit, you know." He gave a dry chuckle at his friend's bemused expression.

Carter shrugged. "I didn't think you'd leave London."

There was something about the way he spoke that concerned Tristan.

He'd missed something, and Carter was hinting at whatever it was.

"Yes, well, I had my reasons for leaving. Is my father waiting for me?" he asked.

"He is, but he doesn't know you've arrived."

Which meant they had a few minutes to talk before his father would learn of his arrival.

Carter turned and went back into the morning room, where one of the Chippendale desks was littered with schoolbooks and papers. A sleek laptop was powered up, and spreadsheets filled the screen. Carter was hard at his studies, unlike Tristan.

Guilt chipped away at the back of his mind. Despite being born with everything he'd ever desired, the need to earn his place, to prove to himself and his father that he deserved the life he had, was always there. *"Never good enough,"* was what his father said. *Never good enough.* A disappointment, a failure as a son. The words were as harsh as a physical blow.

I should be focused on my studies, like Carter, not obsessing over Kat. Not that it had done him any good, in the end.

"I was in London yesterday evening," Carter said, his lips twitching. "Do you remember seeing me?"

He'd seen Carter? *Yesterday?* With a shake of his head, Tristan took a seat at the table.

"I didn't think you'd remember." Carter's lips broke into a full smile. "But I met *her.*"

"Her?" *What the bloody hell did he—*

No, there was no way he had met Kat.

Carter sat down in the chair across from him. With a slow, deliberate movement he closed the laptop and propped his elbows on the table as he fixed Tristan with piercing blue eyes.

"I met Kat. The woman you said you fucked to within an inch of her life and couldn't get out of your head. The same Kat who happens to be your future stepsister."

Tristan flinched. Sometimes he confided too much in his best friend.

"How did you find out?"

"Brianna called me after you met up with her at the pub. She decided to play her hand at matchmaking after you shared your interesting situation with her. She slipped a heavy allergy pill in your drink to make you a tad helpless, and she called me to help get you home. She knew it wouldn't look good for Kat to see you returning home with another woman, especially one you'd been involved with in the past."

"Bri did that to me?" He couldn't believe it. The thought of Brianna planning something like that was almost funny.

With a wry smile, Carter collected his textbooks and notes in an apparent effort to tidy up. "She guessed, accurately so, that Kat wouldn't let you sleep alone while you were in such a wretched condition. If I had to hazard a guess, I'd say you two shared a bed last night."

A warm flush spread across Tristan's face. Everything in his life was suddenly out of his control.

"Did things not work out between you?" Carter's brows drew together.

Not work out? The woman had cut his soul out of his body and left it drifting in the wind like a lost specter. Things not working out was an understatement he couldn't tolerate.

The frustration of the last few weeks had been steadily building like storm clouds inside him, and finally it rumbled out. With a curse, he kicked a nearby chair, and it toppled over in a crash.

His friend's eyes widened, but he didn't retreat.

"Fuck!" Tristan shoved his own chair back and surged to

his feet, fists clenched. "I'm so bloody sick of everyone manipulating me. This is ballocks! The lot of it!"

The only thing in the world he wanted to control was his own life, and it had never been *his* to live. His father and his future title weighed him down and the pressure was crushing. "If I want to go in there and yell at the old man until my throat bleeds, I'll do it," he snapped.

"But what good does it ever do?" Carter sighed. "You know how he is. No amount of shouting will make him see reason. The best you can hope for is to placate him enough so that he'll leave you alone for the time being. It's worked before, it should work again."

As much as Tristan was loath to admit it, his friend was right. If he went in to see his father like this, he'd likely never be allowed to return to Cambridge. The damnable man would restrict him to the estate with excuses of him having to learn management from a practical angle, and his real goal of leashing Tristan like a spaniel would be achieved.

"I've never seen you like this before," Carter admitted in a low voice. "Am I to understand that this is because you and Kat aren't..."

"No," Tristan growled, then bent over and lifted the chair he'd knocked over. He didn't want to admit to his friend that it was more than just physical with Kat. Simply having sex was one thing, but sharing so much of themselves, they'd passed the point of no return. They couldn't be casual. And she wouldn't fit into his life, not the life his father had so painstakingly crafted for him.

There's no escaping it, and I can't take her with me, not without pitting myself against my father and risking the consequences of his anger. There was so much to lose and so many people who could get hurt if his father wanted to punish Tristan. Yet he would risk everything if Kat would agree to take the chance herself.

"She's afraid to be with me."

Carter's brows raised. "What's stopping her?"

"Our parents. She believes it will cause a problem if they find out we're together. She worries her father will overreact." The truth was too painful. Kat was too afraid to love him.

Carter laughed. "She may be right, you know. Parents are tricky creatures to deal with when it comes to their children. Celia's father glares at me every time I enter the room and makes a point to ask if I've been promoted up from stable boy. The man thinks he can rub my situation in my face and keep me from Celia. And damned if it doesn't work because I can't seem to stay near her long enough to have a conversation. I avoid her because I know I'd end up kissing her, and we both know that would...change everything. I can only imagine how unreasonable an American father might be. They're a lot more vocal about their emotions than we Brits are. They have that saying in America, you know, about fathers meeting their daughters' boyfriends with a shotgun in hand. I'm sure Kat's only trying to protect everyone, including you."

Tristan paced the length of the room, staring without seeing the forest-green walls and the paintings of his ancestors. It was a strange thing to feel torn about one's home. The love of this house was in his blood, but his father had ruined the estate with his pride and arrogance, making it a place full of as many bad memories as good ones. Curling his fingers into his palms, he drew in a deep breath and closed his eyes.

"Give it time, Tristan. Your mother and her father will settle down, and when they do Kat's father might see how good you are for Kat. Who knows...maybe he'll surprise us and stop being a pompous arse." Carter took his seat at the table again, seemingly confident with his strategy.

Lord if it were only that easy. Tristan's father was the true barrier between him and Kat. His mother would accept Kat and, given time, he might win over Clayton...but his own father? Hell would be reporting snowfall before Edward Kingsley would ever let an American pollute the title of Pembroke. His father often ranted about their bloodline being traceable back to King Richard I.

"You have no idea what I'm going through. Being around her and not able to touch her, or even smile, without fearing our relationship will be exposed... It's torture." And he was dying.

He glanced at Carter, and his friend's expression stopped Tristan in his tracks. It was not a look of sympathy, but a look of quiet agony that mirrored his own.

"I don't know a thing about torture? To watch the woman you love across the room and know that the smile she sends your way is the only thing you can have? Because you can't touch her, can't kiss her, can't breathe a word to her of the storm raging inside you? I know *exactly* how you feel." Carter raked a hand through his fair hair and stared into the distance, lost in thought.

"Celia." Tristan didn't have to guess. He'd always known how deeply his friend loved her, but he often forgot because he was absorbed with his own concerns. *I'm a bloody selfish bastard...* It was not a reassuring realization.

"Life is a crock of shit," Carter replied.

It was impossible to disagree. No one should tell them how they could live or who they could love.

"Are you staying here through Christmas?" Tristan asked.

With a slow exhale, Carter nodded. "Father is needed here, and I should stay to help when I can. My absence has put a strain on him."

Carter's confession stirred sympathy in Tristan. Ever since Carter's mother had passed away four years ago, Carter's father, John, hadn't been the same. Mr. Martin was in many ways more the lifeblood of this house and its land than Tristan's father was. Edward respected John, but they didn't have the same bond that Carter and Tristan would have when they took over the estate.

He and Carter would be a team, equals in all but title, and if that had been something he could have shared, Tristan would have happily split it down the middle and handed half to his best friend.

"I suppose I'll be here, as well. Maybe I can convince Celia to pay a visit." He grinned, trying to get his friend to laugh.

"Bastard," Carter muttered, but he smiled as he balled up a piece of scrap paper and chucked it at Tristan.

Ducking from the projectile, Tristan couldn't resist another playful jab at his friend. "She could throw another party, and you two can play manor house."

"I'm going to throttle you in your sleep tonight," Carter warned, his eyes bright with amusement.

As Tristan headed for the door, he got one last parting shot in. "Not if you're dreaming about Celia." He was chuckling all the way down the hall until he reached his father's study. The door was closed so he rapped on the solid oak door.

"Enter." That cold voice cut through the wood as if it were butter. He grasped the knob and turned it, opening the door to a room that had always filled him with dread.

His father was seated at his desk, analyzing a spreadsheet. His dark hair was streaked with silver and gave him a debonair look. But the hard eyes and thin lips, which were twisted down, ruined the features which must have made him handsome years ago. Now his father was better suited to the role of a James Bond villain rather than a hero.

"You're late."

Tristan curled his lip. "You didn't tell me to be here at any particular time."

One dark brow slowly cocked over his father's cold blue eyes. "I know how long it takes to drive from your mother's town house to the estate. You took your time in coming here, boy."

Against his better judgment, Tristan slammed the study door shut and almost snarled, "I'm twenty-five years old. I have my own life. If I wanted to wait an entire day before coming that would have been *my* choice."

"Age does not equal good behavior, Tristan. I expect you to come immediately when summoned."

"Summoned?" That was it. He spun on his heel and flung the study door open again, ready to storm out and shatter the door in its frame. But his father spoke first.

"Your Master's program will be ending this spring. It's time we talked about what's expected of you. I've met with Lord Wolverton, and he agrees we're ready to announce your engagement to his daughter. You can be married to Brianna as early as next fall."

Brianna?

His father was playing that hand so soon?

Tristan halfway turned to face his father. "I will make no such announcement. Brianna won't agree, either."

His father laughed. "It's almost charming how you think you have a choice." The harsh laugh died, and his father scowled. "You don't."

Talking to his father was like interacting with a wall. Tristan weighed his options and decided it wasn't worth debating about Brianna right now.

"How long do you wish for me to remain here?" That was what mattered.

"That remains to be seen." Edward leaned back in his chair. "We have matters to handle and arrangements to make for when you leave Cambridge."

Of course. His father never wanted to simply spend time

with him. Tristan shouldn't feel bitter, not after years of this treatment, but it still felt like a hit to the stomach sometimes.

"You're excused. For now." Edward waved a hand at the door in clear dismissal.

Clenching his jaw, Tristan left his father's study, slamming the door behind him. It released a little of the tension and rage that coiled inside him, but not enough.

Carter emerged from the morning room as Tristan stalked past. "Where are you off to now?" he asked.

Tristan didn't even look his way. "I'm going to get drunk. You're welcome to join me."

Pulling back the sleeve of his sweater, Carter glanced at his watch. "I suppose now is as good a time as any to take a break from my studies."

Tristan laughed. "You do know the semester is over?"

"Best to get a head start for next term."

"You're over-enthusiastic as usual," Tristan teased, but again guilt gathered at the back of his mind. He should be studying, earning the education his father was paying for and proving to the old earl that not everything in his life was given to him; that some things were earned.

Yet he was more focused on Kat than his studies. He should be like Carter, worrying over how to maximize profits on the Pembroke estate's investments.

"You'll catch up. You always do," Carter added softly, sensing the direction of Tristan's thoughts. "Come on, let's go find your father's best Scotch."

Tristan could forget about Kat for one night, couldn't he? He'd drink himself under a table to forget how much he wanted her back in his bed and in his life. She was off-limits, his sweet little Kat.

Forbidden.

ix days.

Six days since Tristan had left her standing at the door of Lizzy's town house as he drove away to his father's estate.

How had she lasted that long without him?

Kat lay in bed, cell phone clasped tightly in her hand as she stared at the photo she'd received from the photographer. Jillian had e-mailed a set of photos that displayed the full story, as she'd called it. Tristan walking up to the glass coffin, kneeling, kissing her, and awakening her.

The last image, *the awakening*, held Kat in thrall and made her heart rip apart at the seams. The tips of their noses were brushing, and their lips were only a breath apart. Their eyes were locked on each other, and the expression on her face... Well, she knew what that look meant.

She wasn't falling anymore.

She'd *fallen*.

Kat loved Tristan Kingsley. It was a new, fresh, frightening love, but it was *love*.

While she dared not question what was in Tristan's heart,

she had to admit the same expression was on his face, too. She thumbed through the photos again, seeing how fairy-tale-like they truly were. A fairy tale that would never come true.

She'd stopped them from having any real happiness because she was afraid of her father's reaction, how it could hurt him. But she was also afraid for herself, of how loving Tristan and someday losing him would hurt. *Badly.*

I'm not the sort of girl that someone like him ends up marrying. I wouldn't know the first thing about being a countess and running an estate. He needs a woman who understands how to live that sort of life. And that's not me.

Kat rested the phone on her chest as she stared up at the ceiling. It was supposed to get easier. Every day without him should've hurt less. But the opposite had happened.

Every breath she took hurt because she missed him. Missed the way he smiled at her, the way he touched her, how he made her feel like she was the only person in the world that mattered. She felt the same about him.

Most people would think it was a wild crush, that she was too young to know what she was feeling. But Kat knew that what she felt for him was real. What she was feeling wasn't going to go away, no matter the time or distance put between them. Denying herself what she wanted wasn't possible. And she wanted Tristan back. *It has to be better to have him now, even if I lose him later, when our lives diverge.*

As awful as she felt right now, it couldn't be any worse to lose him someday in the future. So she might as well give it her all and take the leap of faith.

At least I'll know what it was to love him, if I can convince him to come back.

As she'd come to this decision over the last few days she'd finally summoned the courage to do what he'd said. Even if the heartache killed her in the end, it was worth it to try. It was the biggest risk she would ever take, loving Tristan, but she was, for the first time in her life, brave enough to go for what she wanted.

She lifted her phone back up and texted Tristan one little word that held so much hope and promise.

"Yes."

She watched the screen, waiting for a response. It was nine p.m., and he might be out with Carter, drinking, meeting other women...

That picture of him and Brianna flashed across her mind, and Kat shut her eyes tightly and drew in a steadying breath. He'd promised her that he'd be loyal, but did that still matter when she'd told him no? Now that she'd changed her mind, was it too late?

When nothing had happened after several minutes, she knew it was only going to drive her crazy to wait for some kind of response. What had she expected? An instant call or text? A passionate declaration of love?

I'm an idiot.

She turned off her phone and slunk back down into bed. Depression settled in, and she closed her eyes, despising the fresh ache in her chest, like a gaping hole in her heart.

I'm too late. He must have moved on.

A light rap of knuckles on her door barely elicited a reaction from her. "Yeah?" she said, just loud enough for the person on the other side to hear her.

When her dad stuck his head inside, he glanced around at the dim lighting with a frown. "Can I come in?"

She nodded and continued to stare at the wall, curled up in a fetal position on her bed.

"Kat, are you feeling okay? These last few days you've been so quiet and spending a lot of time alone. This is about me and Lizzy, isn't it? I don't want you to be upset. We can talk about it, if you want."

"I'm okay, Dad. I'm just not feeling great. It's got nothing to do with you or Lizzy, I swear."

Her father came over to her bed and perched on the edge, peering down at her. Worry lines formed around his eyes, making him look older than she wanted him to be.

She didn't move. She felt like she was withering away inside.

"Kat, talk to me. Is this about the boy you mentioned at dinner last week?"

The last thing in the world she wanted to talk to her dad about was her love life, but she could tell by his expression that he wasn't going to let it go. With a weary sigh she finally dragged herself up to sit on the bed, facing him. "I liked him. A lot." *Loved him.* "But I think I messed things up."

Clayton sighed. "Kat, honey, you're a perfectionist. You never mess anything up. I doubt that happened."

"That's *exactly* what happened. He liked me, I told him we couldn't date, and now he's gone." That was the truth, or as close to it as she could get.

"Why did you tell him you couldn't date? You've had a boyfriend before. Ben was a nice kid."

She rolled her eyes. "He's nothing like Ben, Dad." And Ben had always been more like a friend than a boy she'd truly dated. Back then, she'd thought she'd really liked him, but now she knew it hadn't been romantic. There was nothing to compare to the intensity of what Tristan made her feel physically and emotionally. He owned her soul, and she'd never thought such a thing was possible.

Understanding filled his gaze. "Ahh, you think I might not approve of this young man?"

Oh, you definitely wouldn't approve, considering he sleeps down the hall and you're marrying his mother.

Kat bit her lip to keep from letting that slip out.

"He's...older," she hedged carefully.

Her dad frowned. "*How* much older?"

Playing with the covers on her bed, she didn't answer right away.

"Kat, how much older is he?" Her father's tone was suddenly heavy, serious.

"Twenty-five." She waited for the explosion, but it didn't come.

He was silent for a long moment. "You're right. He's too old. You'll have plenty of time to date men that age in a few years. Right now, you should focus on studying and making new friends. I know how hard you worked to get into Cambridge, and the last thing you want to do is jeopardize your education."

Kat was all too aware of how lucky she'd been in getting into Cambridge. She'd slaved over her grades, her after-school volunteer activities, creating the perfect student package. When she'd been accepted, it had been one of the best days of her life. She and her father had gone out to dinner to celebrate. She wouldn't let anyone, not even Tristan, distract her from her studies. But that didn't mean she agreed that Tristan was too old for her.

"If it's just a boy that's got you down, try to forget him, honey. He doesn't sound like a very bright young man if he's not willing to wait around for you." Her father patted her shoulder.

"No," she sighed. "He's brilliant." *When he isn't breaking my heart.*

Thankfully her father didn't say anything else about the mystery man. "Well, get some rest. Christmas is a few days away. Lizzy says her cook makes a fantastic Christmas pudding."

At the look of utter delight on her father's face she had to smile, despite her inner aching for Tristan. "Dad, you know that Christmas pudding isn't actually pudding, right?"

"Yes, of course I know that." Her father's tone was mockingly imperious, but a hint of humor in his eyes told her he was teasing. "I'm glad to see you smiling again." He leaned down and brushed a kiss on her forehead.

"Good night, Dad."

"Good night, Kat."

He left her alone, and she lay in bed another fifteen minutes before she caved and turned her phone back on. Still no messages.

Kat tossed her phone on the bed and got up. Maybe a hot shower would help her relax. Every single muscle hurt from the tension she'd been under the last six days. As she exited her bedroom, she took a minute to study the hallway leading to the bathroom.

She hadn't thought much about Lizzy's beautiful house. It was a blend of modern and antique in its interior design and style. She'd barely noticed it before. Tristan had been the sole focus of her attention. Again that little stab of pain through her heart reminded that her she was alone and hurting.

When she got to the bathroom she closed the door. The silver knobs were cold beneath her fingertips as she cranked the hot water on. It was frigid at first, and she let out a little hiss, drawing her hand back from the water.

She stripped out of her pajamas and kicked them into a pile on the floor before she tested the water temperature again. It was perfect. She slid the glass door open further and slipped inside. The glass fogged with steam, and Kat drew patterns on the glass while she let the hot water coat her whole body, warming her up.

Then she tilted her head back and soaked her hair, closing her eyes. She mentally tried to wash away the hurt, the pain, the crushing blow of Tristan's rejection. Not sending a text back to her was a pretty clear way of telling her they were over.

Was this how he'd felt when she'd told him to leave her alone after seeing his picture in the paper with Brianna?

A sound startled her out of her thoughts. She opened her eyes and wiped at the shower door, then gasped.

Tristan stood just outside the stall, staring at her through the misted glass.

Am I dreaming? Please don't let this be a dream...

Kat needed him to be here, with her, so badly she thought she was hallucinating. She was afraid to blink and make it all vanish.

"Tristan?" she whispered.

He said nothing as he gripped the hem of his light gray sweater and pulled it up over his head, exposing his perfect, muscled torso to her gaze. His pec muscles flexed, and his abdominals clenched as he dropped his sweater and reached for the fly of his jeans.

Unable to tear her eyes away from the sight of him through the glass of the shower door, Kat licked her lips. He toed off his boots, stripped off his pants and boxers. He had the kind of body that a woman could stare at for days. It was a body made for touching, stroking, kissing. Every rigid plane of muscle, sloping indentation, and rope of steel was made for a woman's hands.

Tristan Kingsley was designed for seduction. All it would take was one crook of his finger, a lick of his lips, and that suggestive smirk to make her insides quiver and wet heat to pool between her thighs. He was sin personified, a god of lust and desire. *Irresistible.*

Without a word, he gripped the stall door and slid it open. She ducked into the opposite corner, suddenly shy. When they'd made love before it had been dim and beneath the covers. He'd never seen her so exposed. The flare of her hips and breasts seemed huge and embarrassing. A shower was so...intimate. What if he didn't like her all wet and looking like a drowned cat?

"Kat," he rasped in soft admonishment. Gloriously naked, and fully aroused, he slipped into the shower and closed the door, sealing them in a cocoon of heat. He crowded her against the tile, his muscular body a wall of temptation.

This was going to happen. After six days of aching for him, he was here, and he wasn't going to let her go.

❧ 12 ❧

"You got my text?" she asked in a tiny, shy whisper.

He hadn't ignored me. He's here.

Tristan reached around her to adjust the shower nozzle so the spray washed down her shoulders and his lower chest.

"*Yes.*" His answer was an echo of her message. He shattered the stillness of her heart when he reached for her, pulling her to him for a kiss.

Her heart began to pound again as though it hadn't dared to beat in years. Now that he was back, she felt as though were breathing again for the first time in days. She grasped his shoulders, meeting his fire with some of her own.

When they broke apart, both panting, she finally found the words to speak.

"I thought you weren't coming when you didn't reply." She wanted so badly to touch him, explore his skin and let his strength and heat surround her.

Tristan lifted her hands and placed them palms down on his chest. He curled his arms around her waist and pulled her flush against him. Heat exploded through her at the erotic meeting of their naked bodies, the exquisite way their wet skin slid against each other's. It felt too good to be in his arms again.

"I didn't reply because I immediately dropped everything to get to you. The past six days have been hell, Kat. Absolute hell." The stark pain in his gaze floored her. She'd started to wonder if he hadn't wanted her as much as she'd wanted him. But here he was, proving he still desired her, and no one else. And she felt foolish for doubting him.

She slid her arms up around his neck and pressed her right cheek to his chest. His heartbeat thumped softly, reassuring her that he was here with her. Not in a dream.

"Tell me this isn't just sex between us," she whispered, clinging to him as the hot water flowed around them.

The gentle sensation of his lips in the crown of her hair made her feel cherished.

"No, darling. It's more than that. And it scares the bloody hell out of me, but we have to find out where this goes. I don't care if my father has other plans for me. I want to be with you. *Only you.*" The hint of surprise in his tone was reassuring. Tristan was just as startled by his feelings as she was by hers.

There was no denying that. They'd come too far to let go of what was between them.

She lifted her head and nuzzled his throat before kissing a path upward. When she reached his mouth, his lips curved against hers, and it warmed her even more than the hot shower.

"Let me show you how much I missed you. Please," he begged in a gruff whisper. "Then we can take all night and go slow. But it's fucking killing me not to be pounding into you hard enough to make my ballocks ache." His words, roughly uttered, dirty and yet strangely comforting, obliterated any last bit of hesitation.

"Yes, God, yes," she begged.

The low growl that rippled through him flowed into her. He tore a condom from its wrapper and rolled it on.

"Fuck, darling, I'm so close to losing it. I need to be inside you, fucking you until we both hurt from it." The way he said *hurt* didn't sound like a bad thing. She wanted to feel well loved, maybe even a little sore, like she had that first night they'd been together. They'd come together in an explosion of pleasure and power, and she'd liked how she'd felt afterward.

"You make me want to be bad," she confessed between kisses, unable to keep from smiling. "Show me how." It was so true. He took the good girl she'd always been and turned her inside out, making her want to expose that secret part of herself she'd never known until she'd kissed him that night in the pub.

"It will be my sweetest pleasure." The devilish grin he flashed shot a bolt of desire straight to her clit.

He gave her no further warning. Suddenly, Kat was spinning as he rotated her to face the wall farthest from the shower nozzle. He was behind her, caging her against the tile with his body. Tristan kissed her neck and shoulders while his hands slid up from her hips to cup her breasts. Squeezing, kneading them, he played for a few minutes, teasing her until she was wet and begging for him to take her.

"Please, Tristan." She tried to reach back to grab him.

"Keep your hands on the wall, love."

It made her hot as hell when he told her what to do. It gave her freedom to enjoy him and the pleasure he gave her without worrying about what to do.

One of his hands dipped between her thighs, parting her slick folds. "So wet for me, aren't you, little Kat," he purred in her ear just before he nipped the lobe.

It was just the right zing of pleasure in the right spot that made her whimper.

"Tell me," he ordered. "Tell me who makes you this wet, love." That accent, so cultured, so refined, was now low, whiskey rough, and it made the inner muscles in her channel contract.

"You, Tristan, only you." She leaned forward, pressing her head against the cold tile as he played with her, exploring her, inserting one finger into her sex, curling it so that he rubbed against a secret ridge that made her suck in a breath and jerk against his hand.

"There?" he asked, lightly caressing that area inside her again.

"Hmm," was all she could get out.

He swirled his finger around, then began to thrust it harder, hitting that spot over and over again. The climax snuck up on her, then slammed through her like a train. A deep moan of shock and pleasure escaped her lips, and her knees trembled.

"We're just getting started, darling." Tristan kissed a sensitive spot on her neck before he bit down, the hint of pain heightening her pleasure and drawing out aftershocks of her climax.

While she tried to catch her breath in ragged pants, he nudged one of his knees between her thighs and then kicked her feet apart.

"Bend over a little," he urged, roughly gripping her hips. Then he used one hand to guide the thick crown of his erection into her. He bent his knees, and with a hold on her shoulder and on her hip, he shoved into her hard. The shock of his penetration made her cry out, the sound echoing on the tile.

"Shhh," he rasped. "Can't wake the parents." Something about the way he said it, making their actions feel forbidden, made it burn that much hotter.

Tristan ground his hips against her ass, teasing her with an overflow of sensations as he buried his shaft inside her to the hilt. She kept her hands braced on the tile, panting his name over and over again.

"Stop teasing me and just fuck me!" Kat had never begged like that or used such language before she met him. He was a bad influence. A wicked, sexy influence.

He didn't need to be told twice. He withdrew until the tip of him was barely inside her, then he rammed back into her.

Fast. Hard. The almost brutal pace felt so good. It was nearly punishing, his domination of her body, but there was no pain, only hard, intense pleasure. When she came apart it felt like she burst into individual atoms, only to come crashing back together. Tristan muffled a shout behind her, thrusting one last time into her, groaning low.

Kat turned her head and pressed her cheek against the cool tile, sucking in air. Her legs shook, and she started to collapse, but Tristan caught her by the waist and lifted her up so she was leaning back against his chest. He was still inside her, that point of intimate connection making up for the week they'd spent apart.

Tristan kept one arm around her waist, the fingers of his other hand gently curled around her throat, stroking her skin. In the soft rushing water, they were immersed in heat and silence, broken only by their shared breaths.

"You're killing me, love. Every time you banish me from your bed, it destroys me." His lips tickled her ears as he spoke.

"I'm so sorry, Tristan."

I can't live another minute without you. The words were too much to say to him. He'd gotten under her skin and into her heart.

"All is forgiven." He kissed her neck, his hands gentle but firm as he caressed her body. "Let's wash and go to bed."

Kat nodded, her entire body quaking with exhaustion,

relief, and giddiness. Tristan was here, and he'd forgiven her for pushing them apart. Tomorrow she'd worry about the consequences. Tomorrow she'd figure out how they would keep their relationship from being discovered by their parents. Tonight she was going to enjoy being with him and not worry about anything.

Without saying another word, they took turns washing each other. Kat explored his muscles, stroking him as she lathered soap over his skin. Tristan nuzzled her neck, the kisses sweet and tender, sending shivers through her. If only they could stay here, together forever, hot water coating their skin and their bodies pressed close.

Tristan gently washed her hair, his fingers threading through the strands and massaging her scalp in a way that made her entire body hum with contentment.

I've made the right choice. He's worth the risk. She just had to hope now that he wouldn't break her heart.

He exited the shower first, letting her have more than one drool-worthy view of his tight ass and muscled back as he retrieved two thick, fluffy bath towels from the towel rack. He wrapped one around his waist, leaving his happy trail of dark hair exposed. Kat sighed. She was really sleeping with this man.

It was too good to be true, but what fun was there in denying a dream? Sure, it would be safer for her heart to bury what she was feeling and keep her distance. But being with him, as a lover, as a friend... It was no longer something she could pretend she didn't need.

Tristan wound the second towel around her, his expression so serious that the happy little smile on her own lips slipped.

Kat clasped the towel tightly. "What's the matter?" she asked, watching him, her stomach knotting inside.

"You cannot do that to me ever again, Kat. Promise me.

You're the only thing in my life worth fighting for, and I cannot lose you."

The confession was a desperate plea, and the look in his eyes... Oh, her sweet Tristan. It undid her to see him so hurt all because of her. She couldn't keep hold of her own feelings, not when he was willing to open himself up to her.

"I promise. I need you too, so much." Her heart raced.

She had to have Tristan in her life. She hadn't made it six days without him before she'd caved and begged him to come back.

Tristan gripped her shoulders. "Promise you'll never push me away again. I need to hear you say it." His eyes were like a midnight sea, dark and fathomless.

She swallowed the emotions that threatened to choke her. "I promise." Kat meant it. Whatever would happen between them now, it wouldn't end by *her* pushing him away.

Tristan dragged her into his arms, the tight embrace making her feel whole.

"Are you ready to go to bed?" he asked.

"Yes. Take me to bed." She kissed his bare shoulder.

He chuckled. "We'll use your room. It's easier to explain if I'm missing from my bed, but not you from yours."

"Okay." She followed him to the bathroom door.

He unlocked it, opened it a crack, and stuck his head out a few inches.

"We're clear." Tristan grasped her hand, and they dashed down the hall to her room. He tugged her inside, eased the door shut, and clicked the lock into place. Then he smiled at her. "Now, let's get you into bed." He lunged and, before she could react, pulled at the hem of her towel. She spun, trying to evade his hold, but it only ripped the towel clear off her body.

Kat shrieked, then slapped a hand over her mouth. The

last thing she wanted was to wake their parents. Ducking behind the bed, she tried to hide her naked body.

"Come here, Kitty Kat," Tristan teased, stalking toward her, his hands raised, fingers slightly curled in mock claws.

A laugh escaped her. She loved how playful he could be, how it made her feel wild and free. But she didn't want him to catch her just yet. Turning around, she planned to make him chase her, but she stumbled, hit the bed, and fell flat on her back.

Tristan pounced, crawling up her body, but then he rolled them so she lay on top, his own towel falling away, leaving them damp and skin-to-skin.

"Ride me, nice and slow," he whispered, gripping her hips gently.

Nerves released butterflies in her belly. "How do I..." Heat rushed to her face, and she hoped he wouldn't notice her embarrassment.

He moved one hand between their bodies. "Raise your hips."

She did as he said, and then she felt him position himself at her core. He kept one hand on his shaft, easing her down on top. A groan escaped her lips as he filled her completely.

"Oh, God, you're too big," she panted, straining to accommodate him.

Tristan chuckled. "I've fit before, darling. It's just a new position, that's all. Take it as slow as you need to." He smoothed his fingers along her hips, the loving touch melting her inside and relaxing her.

How could he be so sweet? This wicked god in the sack was such a walking contradiction that she couldn't help but be endlessly fascinated with him.

When she was fully seated, he shifted his own body up so he was sitting on the edge of the bed, with her straddling him, impaled on his cock. He banded his arms around her back, holding her chest-to-chest. It was the perfect position for them to kiss. She leaned into him, curling her arms around his neck and bringing her mouth to his. He sighed, the sound full of masculine satisfaction, before he used his tongue to part her lips.

The fire that sparked between them reminded Kat of when he'd entered the pub the night they'd first met. They'd stood so close at the bar, sharing secrets and smiles. Everything inside her had reached out to connect to him. Just like that night, there were electric currents and tingles of invisible fire surrounding them.

Their tongues continued to dance, twirl, flick, in slow, sensual movements, creating a new hungry heat coiling deep in her belly. Soon Kat didn't mind how tight he felt inside her. The more relaxed she became, the more aroused she became. She began to rock her hips, desperate to feel the friction of him moving within her.

"That's it," he murmured between kisses, his encouragement making her feel bold enough to ride him harder. A new pulsing began in her womb, and Tristan responded by fisting one hand in her hair, lightly holding her head steady so he could kiss her deeply while fucking her.

"Does this have to end?" she asked him, riding higher and higher on a building wave of arousal and passion.

Tristan kissed her again, a lingering melting of lips until they were so connected that she couldn't remember ever being apart from him. Her chest ached as it swelled with love. That emotion she'd so feared at the beginning she now embraced, in all its madness and folly.

I love Tristan Kingsley. Come what may, I do.

"If you stay here with me," Tristan whispered, "I can make it last forever. But you have to *stay*."

Could he do as he promised? Make every second a breath of magic, a whisper of an endless thrill? She gazed into his eyes, letting the blue-green shade engulf her. If anyone could make a fairy tale come true, it would be Tristan.

"I'll stay," she promised and raised her hips again, bracing her hands on his shoulders, digging her nails into his skin as she rode him faster.

He moaned her name and that tore her apart. They climaxed together, kissing, both their mouths trembling as they shook and struggled for breath. Kat clung to him, burying her face in his neck as her body relaxed. She was too exhausted to stay awake much longer.

"Sleep," he urged.

She mumbled something as he helped her under the covers. The moment her head hit the pillow she was lost in dreams of falling snow, glistening red apples, and the sweet taste of Tristan's kiss.

TRISTAN DOZED IN THE EARLY MORNING HOURS, PLAYING with a lock of Kat's hair. Suddenly, her cell phone buzzed on the nightstand. He wouldn't have touched it, but it kept buzzing, and he didn't want her to wake up. Reaching over, he grabbed her phone. The screen was lit with a text message from her friend Lacy.

"OMFG, Kat, turn on the TV right now. You're on the news."

Tristan frowned, set the phone down, and reached for the remote. He clicked on the flat-screen, which sat on a stand opposite Kat's bed, and hit the mute button. He scanned the various channels and then bit off a vicious curse.

Jillian, the photographer, was standing in front of Harrods. Behind her was a three-story- tall hanging poster of him and Kat, their lips locked in a kiss, snow falling around them as she awakened in her glass coffin.

Glittering spots covered part of the photo, an effect Jillian had likely edited in, along with an elegant font that read, *"Some loves last forever,"* beneath the haunting, fairy-tale scene. Tristan hit the closed-captioned button so he could read what they were saying.

A beautiful blonde news anchor from the *Daily Mail* was standing next to Jillian. "Your photo was chosen as the fairy-tale campaign winner, and all of the money will be sent to charity, correct?"

Jillian grinned. "Yes. It's a wonderful project."

"This photo and others from the scenes will be part of a Harrods ad campaign all over London. How does it feel to have your work so prominently displayed?" The anchor smiled at Jillian.

Tristan was barely listening. All he kept hearing were the words *"all over London."*

"The subjects of your series have also garnered some public interest. The prince in your photo appears to be none other than Tristan Kingsley, the son of the Earl of Pembroke. He has quite a reputation as a playboy, so it's interesting to see him portrayed like this. Who is the woman he's kissing?"

Jillian coughed politely. "That's not really something I can discuss at the moment." Her gaze darted nervously away from the camera.

"Is that because they're in a relationship?"

"Er..." Jillian's cheeks flushed a bright scarlet. "I can't comment on any of that."

"Oh." The news anchor quickly recovered. "So these displays will be around through the end of February of the coming year?"

"Yes." Jillian beamed again, clearly more comfortable with this topic.

The remote dropped from his hand as he gazed at the screen in shock. Jillian had assured him that the photos wouldn't be leaked; she'd only mentioned that a winning photographer would choose a charity. He'd foolishly assumed that meant she wouldn't have allowed the photos to be publicly promoted at her own desire. The cunning woman had left that part out of their discussion.

He would never have agreed to the shoot if he'd known this would happen. A picture of them lip-locked like there was no tomorrow was going to be everywhere in London. Because the press had recognized him in the photo, it would hit *every* major paper, tabloid, and news outlet in hours, which meant that his father would see it, but worse than that, his mother and Kat's father would see it...

"Bloody hell."

He and Kat were royally fucked.

TURN THE PAGE FOR A QUICK WORD FROM ME AND TO start reading the final installment of Kat and Tristan's story in *Climax*!

The best way to know when a new book is released is to do one or all of the following:

Join my Newsletter:

http://laurensmithbooks.com/free-books-and-newsletter/

Follow Me on BookBub:
https://www.bookbub.com/authors/lauren-smith

Join my Facebook VIP Reader Group called Lauren Smith's League:
https://www.facebook.com/groups/400377546765661/

Turn the page to read the first 3 chapters of *Climax: Love in London Book 3*! Come on, you know you want to turn that page...

CHAPTER 1

"They're not going to find out about us." A deep masculine voice cut through Kat Roberts's muddled thoughts.

She jerked her gaze away from the street view through the town house's kitchen window. It didn't feel like home, but it was her father's fiancée's house, and she would be coming here for future holidays while studying at Cambridge. She would have to get used to it, even the servants appearing around the corner unexpectedly. Maybe after a while it would feel like home if she spent enough time here.

"Kat." That voice, with its sexy British accent, was the reason she'd gotten into this mess. That voice and its owner were completely irresistible, impossibly seductive.

A tall, dark, and sexy dream. No woman could resist that. She hadn't been able to. Since their kiss in the middle of a pub one snowy night, she'd been falling hopelessly in love with him more and more each passing day. With a man she couldn't have.

Tristan Kingsley. He was a twenty-five-year-old bad boy, a business student at Cambridge, and the future Earl of

Pembroke. He was a heartbreaker, and she couldn't stay out of his bed. But most importantly, he was her future stepbrother. Her father had just gotten engaged to his mother, and they were planning their wedding, much to Kat's and Tristan's dismay.

If Dad finds out I've been sleeping with my future stepbrother...

Tristan cleared his throat. "Don't worry. I promise no one will know."

When she looked his way, her mouth went dry and her tongue stuck to the roof of her mouth, making it hard to form words. He always had that effect on her, and she finally understood that expression about a man being a tall drink of water. He made her thirsty just looking at him.

He was leaning one hip against the kitchen counter, arms crossed over his chest. The black trousers showed off his long, muscled legs, and the white dress shirt he wore was unrestrained by a tie, the open collar revealing his throat. She loved to grip that collar when she dragged his head down for a kiss. She glimpsed the sensitive patch of skin she'd spent last night kissing because it made his hips jerk when he was inside her. But her feelings for him were so much more than just physical.

There was something about him, the way he stood at ease, yet every part of his body was hard as steel, like he carried the burden of the responsibility for others on his shoulders. Tristan tried to hide that part of himself when he was with her, but she sensed it was never far from the surface. His sculpted features were undeniable in their beauty and brought to life by his intense, often quiet study of the world around him. He had an air that said he was a cut above others, but what she'd thought was arrogance was actually confidence. She loved that he wasn't afraid to be himself in a world that put too much pressure on a person being someone they weren't. His strength gave her strength, too, which was something she desperately needed after yesterday.

When they'd gone to Harrods to buy a Christmas tree for his mother's town house, paparazzi had tracked Tristan down inside the store. Kat had been overwhelmed by the flashing cameras and questions shouted, but Tristan had kept his calm, and they'd hidden in a broom closet until the reporters lost them.

She'd tasted the pressures of Tristan's position and the nonstop involvement of the news in his personal life. It was apparent that she didn't fit into his glittering world of titled men and women with grand estates, lofty expectations, and an existence that was open to public scrutiny.

Yet when they kissed...well, it was a case of a match meeting a keg of gunpowder, and all the fears and worries of not belonging with him faded away. She just went up in flames whenever he touched her. No man had ever made her feel so wild...so alive. She couldn't walk away from him, even knowing how risky their situation was. She and Tristan weren't blood related, but her dad would freak out if he found his nineteen-year-old daughter sleeping with a man like Tristan. He was a notorious playboy who'd broken hearts and spent nights in the beds of some of London's most famous bachelorettes.

He was her sex god. The man who made every hot, wild fantasy come true. And she was not supposed to be with him.

It was a nightmare.

"What are we going to do?" Kat slumped into a chair at the kitchen table. The house was quiet this early in the morning, except for the occasional creaks and groans of the wood settling.

"We'll explain the photos, but we'll keep the truth about us buried." Tristan pushed away from the counter and took the chair beside her. It seemed so easy for him to talk about hiding their relationship. She knew he didn't take this as seriously as she did. She was falling in love with him, but he wasn't in love with her. This was more of a game for him, a sexy game of hide-and-seek. But the stakes were too high now. Their dirty little secret had just gone public because of the photos.

The photos.

If only there hadn't been evidence, they might've kept their relationship secret a little while longer. A photographer named Jillian had talked them into portraying Snow White and Prince Charming in a fairy-tale-themed charity photo competition at Harrods department store. The set had been lifelike, a glass coffin shimmering with frost and snow. She'd rested her head on a white satin pillow and lay waiting for Tristan to kiss her awake. As magical as that experience had been for her, the fallout had been worse than she could have imagined.

The photographer had led them to believe the winning photo would not be made public and that the stills would be seen only in her portfolio. Early this morning, the winner had been announced on TV. Their photo in a snowy glen, their mouths a hairsbreadth apart from a kiss, their eyes locked in desire and longing, with SOME LOVES LAST FOREVER beneath them, was going to be plastered on every flat surface in London from bus stops to billboards.

How would she explain this to her dad? The last thing Kat wanted to do was create a problem between her father and Tristan's mom.

"Did you call Jillian?" she asked Tristan.

"I did call her. She said it would blow over soon. She didn't think they'd do a news feature about it." Tristan scrubbed a hand though his dark hair and sighed. "Maybe we'll get lucky and Prince Harry will visit Las Vegas again and the press will chase him for a bit and lose interest in us." Tristan's laugh was hollow.

Her heart gave a little tug inside her chest. He looked defeated and anxious. From the moment she'd met him, he'd been cool and seductive and playful. A force of nature in some ways. Nothing had cut through that hardened bad-boy exterior.

Until me. She'd pushed him away twice, trying to deny the intense attraction between them, but she'd only made them both miserable. She'd decided that being with Tristan was worth all the consequences, so she'd asked him to come home from his father's estate. They'd spent all night in bed. It was the kind of lovemaking that changed a person's life forever.

Then they'd woken up to this nightmare. Jillian's photo was everywhere, and the story was out. Their parents would connect the dots.

"We'll tell them a half-truth." Tristan reached under the table and placed a reassuring hand on her thigh. It was a sensual touch, but she could see in his eyes he wasn't thinking about sex.

The wildfire that burned between them was unstoppable, and the intensity had deepened in a way she'd never imagined. The attraction that had drawn her to him like a moth to a flame was growing. Her beautiful, brooding Tristan, with his guarded heart, was trying to comfort her. It wasn't just about sex anymore. Even if he didn't love her, he cared for her, and that was enough for now. And that was why she adored him, because even though the lust burning between them was unrelenting, he also cared about her, proving that he wasn't just thinking about sex, not when she was worried about other things.

How do we get out of this mess?

"What will we tell them?"

"We couldn't say no to a charity event. We just did what

the photographer told us to." He leaned over and pressed his lips against her neck. Tiny waves of comfort from that slow, tender brush of his mouth overrode her panic, if only for a moment. Tristan's kisses made her fall through time and space until she lost herself in his private universe.

"I'll tell them first thing. If we're open about it, they won't think we're hiding anything. Trust me, Kat." He cupped her face, and just like that, she was trapped in his blue-green gaze.

"I trust you." And she did.

"Good." He pressed a featherlight kiss to her lips, then jerked away as the kitchen door opened.

Tristan's mother, Lizzy, stood there, eyes darting between the two of them. Her long blond hair was pulled back in a fashionable chignon and she was dressed for the cold weather, her gloves damp with snow and her boots shiny with water.

"Tristan! When did you get back? I thought you were going to stay with Edward for the remainder of the holidays."

"Well, I was half-tempted to tell Father to stuff it, but then I decided I didn't care to speak to him about it all and just came back here without telling him. I'd much rather be with you for Christmas."

Lizzy's shoulders dropped in relief. "I hope your father doesn't get too angry."

They all hoped that. Tristan's coldhearted father was continually dragging Tristan home to the Pembroke estate whenever it suited him, regardless of Tristan's plans. He'd risked his father's fury coming home earlier than he promised, and Kat still feared that Tristan would suffer for it.

"I saw the most unusual...photograph this morning." Lizzy's face turned red as her gaze darted to Kat and then back to her son, betraying the nature of her thoughts. She fidgeted slightly, her lips parting as she licked them nervously.

Kat blinked, then swallowed hard as she took in Lizzy's

attire and realized Lizzy must've already gone out, which meant she had seen...

Tristan stood, smoothed his sweater, and offered his mother a smile. "You saw the charity photograph, didn't you? You see, it's quite the story. Kat and I were Christmas tree shopping, and a photographer begged us to be models for the shoot. We felt obligated to aid her, for charity, of course. Isn't that right, Kat?" His tone implied she ought to join in their little game of secrets.

Secrets. She hated them, but she wanted Tristan, at any cost.

Kat got to her feet, keeping a safe distance from Tristan, even though she wanted to reach for his hand.

"Yes. Jillian was very sweet. We couldn't turn her down, even when she told us we'd have to reenact Snow White. We're happy she won the contest. There were two other photographers involved in the fairy-tale photo shoots." She did her best not to sound too falsely excited.

"Oh?" Lizzy's voicing of that one syllable seemed to be a challenge—not a threatening one, but a worried one.

"Yes, the whole situation was far too awkward, but we endured it for the sake of charity, didn't we, Kat?" Tristan walked over to the fridge as he spoke and retrieved a pitcher of orange juice, calmly pouring himself a glass.

Lying seemed so easy for him, but it wasn't for her. Her palms got sweaty and she licked her lips every time Lizzy looked at her.

"Well, it was certainly nice of you to help with something that goes toward a good cause." Lizzy continued to stare at Kat, her brow furrowed, apparently deep in thought, but she was stopped from saying anything further when Kat's father strolled into the kitchen.

He was smiling and humming.

"Only one day until Christmas," he announced, and

leaned over to press a kiss to Lizzy's cheek before he hugged Kat. "Morning, sweetheart." Then he nodded at Tristan. "Tristan, back from your father's for Christmas?"

"Yes. I got in late last night and didn't want to wake anyone." Tristan inclined his head; then his gaze darted to Kat.

"Everyone have their shopping done?" Clayton asked.

Lizzy cleared her throat. "Actually, I need to grab a few things. Kat, would you like to join me?"

"Mum, I could take you—" Tristan took a small step toward his mother, as though to protect Kat from her.

"I'd love to go," Kat said. With a hand on Tristan's hip, she nudged him aside. He moved reluctantly. If she had to pick a parent to be around for the next few hours, Lizzy was a lot less scary than her dad when it came to keeping her secrets.

"Kat, how much time do you need to get ready? I'm able to leave as soon as you are." Lizzy already held a casual black clutch purse in one hand.

"A few minutes. I just need to grab my shopping list." She glanced at her father and then Tristan before bolting for the door.

Heart racing, she ran up the stairs and slid to a halt just inside the room. Blood pounded in her head, drumming against her temples. Keeping secrets had never been a talent of hers. She'd never had actual secrets to safeguard before, and now she had the mother of all secrets building into a violent storm inside her.

The question was, who would survive the fallout?

She'd taken two steps farther into her room, when a hand settled on her waist from behind and she sucked in a little shriek. Another hand clamped around her mouth, cutting off the sound. A tall, lean, muscled body pressed against her back.

"Shh...You have to calm down, Kat." Tristan's too-sexy

accented voice rumbled against her right ear, his breath tick-ling the fine hairs on her skin. He was so warm...and hard behind her. The pounding of his heart tapped against her back between the thin layer of their clothes, and she felt that inexorable pull toward him.

Like gravity. God, the man was the personification of sinful temptation. She never stood a chance.

He dropped his hand from her mouth. He dominated her whenever he touched her, and she craved that more than anything. She leaned back against him, absorbing his heat and strength. Being with him, even secretly, made her feel so alive, so feminine and sexy, but it wasn't just about the sex.

From the start she and Tristan had been connected on a level she'd never thought possible. It hadn't been love at first sight—she didn't believe in that—but it had been obsession at first sight. Something about him pulled her in, like a whirlpool in the Amazon River, drawing her deeper and deeper into him. Now she was unable and unwilling to escape. He'd let her have a glimpse into his soul, and she'd fallen hard and fast. It was a dangerous thing to be in love with Tristan Kingsley.

He shut her bedroom door and flicked the lock before leaning back against the closed door. When he crooked one finger in silent invitation, she closed the small distance between them. Tristan's arms wound around her waist as he tugged her tight to his body and dipped his head.

The slight pause before he kissed her was sensual torture. She wanted his mouth on hers, and he loved to tease her, make her wait even a second more than she wanted to. When his gaze traveled from her eyes down to her lips, she rocked up on her tiptoes, kissing him first like she had the night in the pub when they'd met.

Kat drank in the taste of him as their lips met. Electricity pulsed beneath her skin, humming softly with every feathery caress of his mouth on hers. She couldn't help but think of that line from *Romeo and Juliet* "Thus with a kiss I die…" How true it felt. This kiss stopped her heart for a second too long, and she spiraled into a world of need and hunger that knew no limits. There was no life outside his kiss.

A shiver of longing rippled through her. She needed more…and she needed fewer clothes.

Tugging at his pants, she tried to undo the button on his fly while still kissing him. His hands slid from her waist to her ass, gripping it hard. Spikes of sharp arousal tore through her, and her clit throbbed in little pulses of desire.

"You don't have to go with my mum." He flicked his tongue into her ear and she shivered. "You could stay right here…" Tristan let his words hang in the air with sensual promise as he rocked his hips, pressing against her hands, which were trying to open his pants. There were a hundred things he could do to convince her to stay right where she was, but his words reminded her that Lizzy was downstairs waiting for her. The thought brought her out of the sensual haze she'd been in, and she pulled away from him. Catching her breath, she shook her head, feeling foolish that he always derailed her when she was trying to be on her best behavior.

"As tempted as I am, I should go. I haven't bought your present yet and Christmas is tomorrow."

Tristan chuckled and rubbed a palm on her stomach. "The only present I want is you unwrapped beneath me in my bed." He kissed her cheek and held on to her for a long moment.

Kat clung to him. "I'd like that a lot, but I do *need* to shop. Spending time with your mom might be a good thing for both of us."

He pulled back so he could stare down at her. "We haven't talked much about our parents' upcoming marriage." He tipped her chin up with one elegant finger, and Kat bit her lip before replying. It stunned her that he had the power to turn a moment focused on sex to something packed with emotion. From the second he'd walked into the pub a few weeks ago, she felt as if she was riding on an emotional roller coaster.

"I'm coping, barely." Her mother had cut and run on her and her dad so long ago that she didn't know how to have a bigger family. "What about you?" she asked. Tristan had always been cool, calm, and collected, almost satirical in his approach to their parents, but he had to be hurting like she was.

For a brief instant, that wall of imperial control descended on his face, but then he softened. "Mum and I...aren't used to sharing each other. I've been the man of the house for a long time, and it's been disconcerting to relinquish most of that control to your father."

"It's definitely not easy to share a parent when you haven't had to before." She snuggled close again. "At least we have each other." The words slipped out before she could stop them.

Tristan made a soft dark noise and leaned down to kiss her hard, in an almost punishing manner before he spoke. "We *do* have each other, and you can't ever leave me again. Do you understand?"

She took in his face, the panic in his eyes and the tension bracketing his mouth. He'd been wounded when she'd called off their relationship. It seemed ironic that she'd gone into this thinking she'd be the one to get hurt, but instead she was the one causing him pain.

"I understand. I'm sorry, Tristan." The words caught in her throat and choked her.

He brushed at her cheeks, and she blushed when his fingertips came away wet with tears. Tristan made a teasing *tsk* noise before pressing another fervent kiss to her lips.

"So you and Mum will go shopping. What am I supposed to do while you're gone?"

She rolled one shoulder in a small shrug. "Bond with my dad?"

His rich laugh warmed her. "Not bloody likely, darling." He was still shaking his head with apparent amusement. "I'll plan something so you and I might have time alone later. How does that sound?"

Pretending to think about it for a minute, she finally nodded and then flashed him a grin. "Sounds nice."

"Excellent." He stole one more quick kiss before he slipped out of her bedroom.

That was the most important thing. Not getting caught together by their parents. Stepsiblings shouldn't be seen making out, and they definitely should not be having hot sex with each other...and she and Tristan had done both.

Dad would kill us if he found out...

CHAPTER 2

A few minutes after Tristan left her room, Kat did the same. She could hear Tristan's voice echo up from the stairs. It sounded like he was talking to her father. She heard the word *Super Bowl* and rolled her eyes.

Her father was a football junkie. No one would know it to look at him; he was a polished, well-dressed investment banker, but when it came to football, he was one step away from painting his face and waving a giant foam finger.

Lizzy met her at the bottom of the stairs, smiling warmly. "The boys are occupied with sports, so we can make our escape."

"I'm ready to take on the last-minute Christmas shopping," she said, grinning as she followed Lizzy out the door.

Tristan's mother smiled back. "Me too. Let's hope the crowds aren't too terrible."

A black Porsche SUV was parked outside, and a driver in a black uniform opened the door as they walked down the slick sidewalk. They climbed into the car and buckled up.

"Where to, Ms. Harlow?" the driver asked as he started the car.

"Paul, take us to Harrods. We're on the hunt for an Aspinal of London briefcase."

The driver glanced at them through the rearview mirror. He was a ruddy-cheeked man who smiled at her. "Of course, my lady."

Lizzy settled her purse on her lap and glanced in Kat's direction as she tugged her black leather gloves off and slipped them into her purse.

For several long minutes neither of them spoke, but Kat couldn't stand the silence. "So, Lizzy..." She cleared her throat. "You need to do some last-minute shopping, too?"

Lizzy smiled. "Yes. I was hoping you might weigh in on a briefcase for your father. I noticed his is a little worse for wear. I was thinking of getting him a new one." She waited for Kat to respond, but the Porsche came to a halt in front of Harrods.

"Oh my..." Lizzy put one hand to her breast as she peered out the window at something.

"What?" Kat leaned toward her, able to see the bottom half of...She sucked in a breath.

The picture of her as Snow White and Tristan as Prince Charming covered an entire side of the department store. A picture that still caused heat to rush to her face and made her light-headed all at once, because it was obvious to anyone looking at that picture that she was in love with Tristan Kingsley. Kat hoped he felt the same about her, that he *loved* her.

"Paul, we'll call when we're ready to be picked up." Lizzy's voice was strangely quiet.

"Very good, my lady," Paul replied before he climbed out and opened their door.

Kat reached the sidewalk and tilted her head back to get a better glimpse of the huge ad.

"Well, that's quite a picture." Lizzy tugged her coat up

around her neck. "I imagine it was an interesting experience to shoot."

She nodded. "We were ambushed by the photographer and she talked us into posing for charity. So we did." Was it pathetic to admit, even to herself, how much she loved looking at the photo? *How did I fall in love with him so fast?* She'd always lived her life cautiously and kept most people at a distance.

Because Tristan wouldn't let me keep my distance. He opened me up and he opened himself up, and now look at us.

"What's the matter, Kat?" Lizzy touched her shoulder, and she came back to herself.

"Sorry. I'm just thinking, I need to get you and Tristan both presents. I hadn't planned for this." Damn, that hadn't come out right. "What I mean was, I didn't know about you until after I'd bought my presents a month ago." She hoped Lizzy understood what she was trying to say.

"It's fine, Kat. None of us planned this. I need to get you a gift as well." Lizzy smiled and squeezed Kat's shoulder. "If you see anything you like, just give me a wink and a nudge."

It was *impossible* to dislike Lizzy. Even though she was still struggling to accept the whole marriage thing, Kat couldn't deny how much she liked the woman her father had chosen.

"Same here—for you, I mean," she added, feeling a little shy but strangely excited. It had been so long since she'd been around a mother. Lizzy wasn't *her* mother, but shopping, just the two of them for a family Christmas, might actually be fun.

"Let's get inside. I'm thinking we should look for briefcases first."

They entered the department store, pushing through the almost frantic crush of holiday shoppers to get to the escalators that would take them to their desired floors. Over the next hour she and Lizzy shopped, not just for the men but for each other and for themselves. They tried on fancy dresses and scarves, even *oohed* and *ahhed* over designer purses, things Kat never thought she'd do, much less enjoy doing. Yet Lizzy had coaxed her into dressing rooms and insisted she try on a dozen things just because she could.

It was *fun*.

Kat bought a blue linen photo album for their wedding photos and any others Lizzy might like to keep. She'd caught Lizzy admiring the album earlier and had a feeling it would be perfect.

Laden with purchases, they met Paul at the car and he dutifully relieved them of their bags and packages, stowing them methodically in the trunk.

"Where to now, Ms. Harlow?" Paul asked as he climbed into the driver's seat.

Tapping a gloved finger against her lips, she looked at Kat. "What else do you need?"

"Something for Tristan."

Lizzy smiled. "Well, I can certainly help you with that."

Kat had been thinking about it all day. It had to be the right thing. Something he loved, something that he would cherish like she did the first edition of *The Mysterious Island* by Jules Verne he'd bought for her a few weeks before.

"I thought I might get him a map. Something old, or at least a reproduction of something old." A map was the most logical choice. He had confessed one night in bed that he was fascinated by cartography.

She'd known that first night he'd never before opened up to anyone the way he had to her. Talk about seduction of the heart, mind, and body...

"How did you know he liked maps?" Lizzy's question sliced through the delightful memories of Tristan's body wrapped around hers as he'd whispered about his dreams and secret joys.

"He...uh..." Words seemed to clog her throat, unable to get free. "He told me while we were Christmas tree shopping."

There. That sounded reasonable, didn't it?

"He did?" Lizzy was openly staring at her now.

Great. She kept forgetting she was supposed to know less about Tristan than she actually did.

"Yeah..." She tried to think fast. "I was telling him about how I liked Russian symphonies, and he said he liked old maps."

"I'm so glad you two are getting comfortable with each other." Lizzy seemed to relax. "Paul, take us to Standfords in Covent Garden."

"Yes, ma'am." The driver pulled out into traffic.

"What's Standfords?" Kat asked.

"A map store, among other things. They have quite the collection of rare map reproductions at good prices."

It sounded perfect. Lizzy had to be some sort of present genius.

The car pulled up in front of a store with bright red painted doors. STANDFORDS stood out in white block letters above the entrance. The windows were brightly decorated with maps, globes, and books about exotic lands like Morocco and Egypt.

Inside the store, Lizzy and Kat wandered the aisles and perused the shelves. Light walnut wood racks had dozens of maps draped over rungs, and small can lights illuminated the endless books along the walls.

Kat trailed a fingertip over each spine of the travel guides as she walked along, not seeing anything that seemed right. She froze when she reached a shelf with navigation tools on it. She found a rosewood box containing an antique brass compass with the year *1818* engraved on the brass cover.

"That's a lovely Brunton," Lizzy said, joining her by the shelf, her keen eyes roving over the compass's features.

"Do you think Tristan would like it?" She held her breath. Lizzy would tell her the truth, wouldn't she?

"Ah, yes, I think so." Lizzy smiled, but then she met Kat's gaze. "Are you and Tristan bonding? I know he can be a bit wild..."

That was an understatement. Tristan was untamable, a sex god that couldn't be ignored or resisted. Sleeping with him had pulled her apart cell by cell and put her back together. He'd *changed* her. Kat had fallen in love with him. *Wild* was definitely not the right word. He made her feel so many different things: new, exposed, and not herself.

"Tristan has been great. He's made me feel very welcome." Kat stroked her fingers over the brass surface of the compass.

He'd told her that he loved maps because they were like windows into the past, seeing how men and women viewed the world. A cultural memory frozen in time. Tristan had made maps seem beautiful, enchanting, and fascinating. But Kat wanted to give him something that would guide him. What good were maps if you didn't have a tool to read them? He needed to find his way in the world, make his own path separate from his father.

"I'm glad he's behaved himself," Lizzy said, but her tone was still serious. "He has a difficult time ahead. Between his father and his future title, he has so much to worry about, and I fear it's affected his relationships." She paused.

Kat held her breath until it seemed to singe her lungs with pain.

"What I mean is that he's not ready to settle down and date women. He's quite a charmer, and many decent women with good heads on their shoulders still vie for his attention, but he isn't serious about any of them. My son has left many broken hearts in his wake." When Lizzy met Kat's gaze, everything in Kat went still.

That sounds like a warning.

Tristan's mother knew about them. She *knew*…Kat tried not to panic, not to overreact or give herself away.

Lizzy placed a hand on Kat's wrist.

"It would be best if Clayton thought Tristan's heartbreaker tendencies wouldn't affect anyone he knew, especially someone he loves so very much." She gave Kat's now trembling hand a little pat and then tapped a finger on the compass. "You should get this for him. He doesn't have one, and I think he'll love it. You have an eye for beautiful things."

Kat glanced down at the compass. *God, please don't let Lizzy change her mind and tell Dad about us…* She didn't think Lizzy would risk upsetting Clayton, but she wasn't sure.

Collecting the compass, she headed to the cashier's desk, her legs shaking a little and her blood pounding in her ears. Everything would be fine; they wouldn't be discovered. She had to keep telling herself that and maybe she'd believe it.

Tonight they would open presents, and tomorrow was Christmas. Her *first* Christmas with her new family. It still hadn't sunk in. She was part of a bigger family now, one that included a stepmother and a stepbrother. The fact that she was sleeping with her future stepbrother…well, she couldn't let herself think about that right now.

As the man at the cash register wrapped up the compass, she noticed Lizzy talking on her phone. Her face was ashen, her grip on the phone white-knuckled.

"Please, Edward. Don't take him from me, not tonight," Lizzy pleaded, her head dropping and her eyes closed. Her fear turned to quiet rage as her lips thinned and her eyes narrowed. "You don't own me anymore. I made that clear when I left. You do not get to dictate what happens to me anymore." Lizzy's eyes opened again, and a steel fury burned in their depths. Then she disconnected the call, her anger flowing out of her as her shoulders dropped.

"Lizzy, is everything all right?" Kat collected her bag and joined Tristan's mother by the shop's entrance.

Slipping her phone back into her purse, Lizzy massaged her eyes and attempted to smile. "Tristan's father thinks he can stop me from marrying your father. He's threatened to keep my son away from me."

"But Tristan's not a child. It's not like you'd have a custody battle. He's twenty-five."

Lizzy shook her head. "It's complicated. Oh, I wish sometimes I'd never married Edward, but then"—she paused and a true smile lit her face—"I see my son, and I would endure that heartache all over again. That's why I named him Tristan."

"What do you mean?" Kat focused on Lizzy's eyes, hating the hurt she saw in the other woman's gaze.

"I didn't know when I married Edward that he was in love with someone else. I was..." Lizzy struggled for words. "A replacement for the woman he couldn't have. I found out a few months into our marriage, before I discovered I was pregnant. I was so happy in so many ways, but I knew I'd never win Edward's heart. Tristan was a child made from that grief. The name *Tristan* is French for *sadness*."

All around them the store was filled with customers, but Kat didn't notice them as she listened to Lizzy talk about something so intimate and personal.

"You named him?"

Lizzy nodded. "Edward wanted a family name, but I won that battle. I stayed with Edward as long as I could to give Tristan as normal a life as I could manage. That's what being a parent is. Making sacrifices to give the best to your child. It's instinct—it's love."

Kat's throat constricted and her eyes stung. Her mother hadn't felt that way about her. If she had...

She wouldn't have abandoned me and Dad.

"Kat?" Lizzy's hand clasped one of hers and squeezed. "I'm sorry if I upset you. I shouldn't have burdened you with these things."

"No—no, it's not that," Kat whispered. "I was just thinking how lucky Tristan is to have you. My mother..." A lump formed in her throat, choking anything else she might've said. But Lizzy was too perceptive.

"I imagine Tristan would feel the same way about you and your father. Clayton is wonderful, nothing like Edward." A rueful little smile curved her lips. "He's the kind of man I ought to have married. I'm glad to have the chance now." A delicate blush pinkened Lizzy's cheeks. "I hope Clayton and Tristan grow close someday. It would do Tristan some good to get to know a man who isn't driven by greed and ambition."

"Have you and Dad set a date for the wedding?" Kat asked.

"Not yet. I'm not sure I want a big wedding, so if your father doesn't want a big one either, we might be able to get married soon. We could even forgo the church and do a civil ceremony."

"You don't want a big wedding?"

Lizzy smiled softly. "No. Marrying your father is what matters. I don't care how it comes about, whether in a church and a white gown, or a simple wedding with just witnesses at the Mayor's Parlour."

Kat suddenly gasped when an idea struck her. "Lizzy, why don't you and Dad just get married today? You can, can't you?" In the short time she'd been around Lizzy, she had to admit the woman was good for her father. She laughed at his silly jokes, and the way she leaned in to him when they hugged and how he beamed down at her...There was true affection there, and her father had lost his tired, haggard look. Her dad was *happy*. What was the point in delaying?

Lizzy nibbled her lip, and then with a tentative smile, she looked at Kat. "Do you think your father would...? I mean, would he miss the fanfare of an official church wedding?"

Kat shook her head. "No, he wouldn't." She knew her dad well enough to know all that would matter was that he married Lizzy, and that Kat was there.

"Well, then, I suppose I ought to call him." With another girlish blush, Lizzy dialed Clayton.

Kat stepped toward the waiting car to give her some privacy, and she pulled out her own phone. After removing her gloves and stuffing them into her pockets, she texted Tristan.

Wedding is happening today. We're coming straight home.

Home. The word felt right now. Lizzy's town house was becoming home, just as Tristan already was.

Her phone vibrated seconds later, and she read the responding message.

Today?

Yes. She tapped her response. Was he going to be upset?

Very well.

Biting her lip, she typed again. *Are you mad?*

Rather than text her back, her phone rang and she answered instantly. "Hello?"

"Kat, as long as you stay with me, I don't care what our parents do. *You* are what matters to me."

She sighed, every ounce of tension in her suddenly evaporating.

"Now, come home so I can show you how much I've missed you." His soft chuckle turned her knees to jelly. How he had the power to do that, she'd never know.

"See you soon." She hung up and saw Lizzy watching her. Those fine lines of worry on her brow were deeper.

"Did you call Tristan?" Lizzy asked.

"Yeah, I thought I'd let him know..." Was she giving their secret away?

"Right," Lizzy said, her eyes still dark with a shadow of concern

She knows.

Lizzy really knows about Tristan and me.

Kat swallowed, faking a smile, and got into the car with Tristan's mother. Her father couldn't find out. Ever.

CHAPTER 3

Tristan straightened his silver tie and took his place beside Clayton. As he studied Kat's father, Tristan had to admit the American cleaned up nicely. They both wore matching black tuxedos with silver waistcoats.

My stepfather. Tristan tried it out in his head. It didn't sound...terrible. The man was a nice fellow after all, and his mother adored him, which was what mattered most. Kat's father shifted restlessly and glanced at Tristan.

"I don't know why I'm so nervous." Clayton laughed.

"You'll do fine," Tristan assured him, but he too felt an odd stirring of nerves inside, as if he were the one getting married, not Clayton.

Kat's father nodded as though to steady his resolve. "I've never been more sure of anything in my life."

This marriage was going to be a good thing for both Clayton and Lizzy. Tristan wasn't blind, and he had noticed the changes in his mother since she had met Clayton. The happy animation of her features, the sunny glow of her smile, and the full laughter whenever Clayton teased her. It reminded Tristan of Kat, her laughter, her smiles.

Reaching out, he shook Clayton's hand.

"Thank you, Tristan. I can't tell you how much it means that you're supportive of our decision to marry. I know things are...rough with your father. I'm here for you, in whatever way you need me."

The genuine honesty in Clayton's face and voice filled Tristan with a strange cottony warmth. He blinked, a little startled by the sensation.

Before he and Clayton could say another word, the door to the Mayor's Parlour opened. The registrar, a short gray-haired man, smiled at them.

"The ladies are ready for you." The man nudged the door open more, letting Tristan and Clayton enter the room behind him.

The Mayor's Parlour was a warm, oak-paneled room in Town Hall, a fashionable Upper Street building that was home to the Registry Office. Vases filled with English wild-flowers covered the tables. The room had red leather armchairs, a couch, and burgundy carpets, along with the grand fireplace that was decorated with a coat of arms above the mantelpiece.

Next to the fireplace, his mother stood in a red knee-length dress with long sleeves and a scalloped bodice. It was an edgy fashion choice, to be sure, but he knew she was done being prim and proper. Her hair was down in soft romantic waves that glinted in the firelight, and the smile on her lips showed only a hint of nerves.

"Wow," Clayton whispered, a boyish grin on his face.

Tristan rolled his eyes. The man acted like a young lad with a schoolboy crush.

"Dad, you look great." Kat's voice pulled his focus away from Clayton, and Tristan's heart gave a little jolt, skipping a few beats.

Kat stood a few feet away from the fireplace in a

sapphire-colored cocktail dress. A thick white silk sash wound around her waist, and she wore white crystal-studded kitten-heeled shoes. Her skirts fluttered around the tops of her knees as she shifted on her feet. Her long brown hair had been pulled back from her face with a few jewel-studded butterfly pins.

He wanted to sink his hands into her hair and kiss her. The urge was so strong that he'd crossed the room and his hands were reaching for her before he'd even realized what he was doing. Catching himself just in time, he dropped his hands to her shoulders in a friendly, brotherly pat before he let go.

"You look wonderful, Kat," he said, forcing the huskiness out of his voice, as their parents were standing only a few feet away.

"Thank you. Your mother picked it out." Kat ruffled her dress while a sweet blush rose to her cheeks.

"Are we ready?" The registrar joined them by the fireplace.

Tristan moved to stand behind his mother, while Kat positioned herself behind her father.

She kept glancing his way, her gray eyes as soft as the down feathers of a mourning dove. When a little smile escaped onto her lips, it knocked him behind the knees.

The woman was his kryptonite. He couldn't resist her, *had* to have her.

Tristan was only vaguely aware of the wedding vows and the exchange of wedding bands. His entire body and mind were focused on Kat.

If he closed his eyes, he'd relive the moment he saw her in the glass coffin, the ruby gown so bright against her creamy skin. She'd been a fantasy, a lover ready to be awakened by his kiss.

When she'd impulsively kissed him in the pub that snowy night in Cambridge, he'd come undone and been reborn. He was done living the way he had, moving from lover to lover. None of it meant anything, and he was tired of feeling that way.

Kat's kiss had swept him off his feet like a rip current off the shore, and he didn't want to fight another second. Not when it meant they couldn't be together.

"I now pronounce you husband and wife." The registrar's declaration broke through Tristan's thoughts, and he blinked, suddenly remembering he was in the middle of his mother's wedding.

Lizzy was kissing Clayton, her lips curving into a smile while he held tightly on to her waist. They looked blissfully happy.

Tristan glanced back at Kat. Her eyes glinted with tears and she sniffed.

"Congratulations, Dad, Lizzy." Kat embraced them both when they broke apart.

"Thank you, Kat." Lizzy was teary-eyed, too, with happy tears.

"Are we ready to go home and eat Christmas Eve dinner?" Clayton clapped his hands together, which made Kat giggle, and her eyes met Tristan's.

"I have quite an appetite." Tristan smiled at her and then licked his lips. Another blush. She could obviously see he'd meant he was hungry for something else entirely.

"Good," Lizzy said. "Mrs. George will have baked up half the kitchen tonight."

Tristan caught Kat's waist when they fell into step behind their now-married parents.

"It's official, little sister," he murmured in her ear as he pulled her close. What he wouldn't give to drag her into the nearest closet and get his hands up her skirt so he could—

"*Stepsister*," she corrected in a breathless hiss so their parents wouldn't hear.

"Who knew this would feel *so bad?*" He squeezed her lightly, feeling the soft fabric of her dress crush beneath his fingers.

"Stop it, please. Not here," Kat begged him, but when her eyes met his, they were blazing with heated desire. She was as twisted up as he was and desperate to get a minute alone with him.

For a brief moment, as the four of them walked through Town Hall, the world seemed full of possibilities. Tristan thought his chest would burst with happiness.

They exited the building, and chaos erupted around them.

Cameras were everywhere, and a massive crowd of reporters were crushing in against them from all sides.

"Elizabeth Harlow, is it true you've just remarried? What does the Earl of Pembroke think about your new husband?" a man with the *Daily Mail* logo on his shirt shouted.

Clayton cursed and stumbled back, protecting Lizzy.

"Mum, the car is straight ahead!" Tristan shouted over the erupting madness of the press, while he covered Kat with his arms. She pressed in to his side and ducked her head.

"Out of the way!" Clayton bellowed, and started shoving men out of his path to the waiting car.

"Mr. Kingsley, is this your new girlfriend? Is she your stepsister?"

Another camera flash, then lights dotted his vision, and he clutched Kat to him, trying to half carry her to the car.

"Tristan!" Kat cried out when someone grabbed her arm, attempting to tug her from Tristan's hold.

Before he could think it through, Tristan reacted and swung a fist, landing a blow on a man's jaw.

The reporter let go of Kat's arm.

"That bugger punched me!" the reporter screeched, but Tristan didn't care as he got Kat and his mother into the car.

Their parents climbed into the middle seat and he and Kat got into the backseat behind them.

"Tristan, you didn't hit him, did you?" Lizzy glanced out the car windows at the flock of reporters still taking photos.

He wrapped an arm around Kat's shoulders and pressed a kiss to her temple. His body was flooded with adrenaline and rage. Tristan was sick of the paps getting in his face, frightening the people he cared about. He would do anything to protect Kat, anything because she meant *everything*.

"Lizzy." Clayton's voice pulled Tristan's attention to the front. Kat's father was half turned around in his seat, staring at them.

"Yes, dear?" Lizzy's nervous gaze darted between her husband and Tristan.

"That reporter said something about Kat and Tristan...*dating?*"

Lizzy swallowed, then laughed. "Oh—that's ridiculous, dear."

Their car turned the corner, leaving the reporters behind, but Tristan cursed as a bus pulled up alongside them. A large ad was on its side. An ad he recognized with dread. Prince Charming kissing Snow White.

"What in the *hell?*" Clayton's eyes widened as he took in the ad, then narrowed to slits as he turned to stare at Lizzy.

Tristan swallowed hard. This was it. They'd been outed before he was ready. A knot tightened in his stomach as he struggled to come up with a new plan. There was no way Kat's father would buy the story they'd told his mother this morning.

"Kat, why are you kissing Tristan on a bus ad?"

"Dad—" Kat tried to pull away from Tristan, but he wouldn't let her go. It was all going to come out and there was no stopping it.

He rubbed the back of his neck as heat flooded his face.

Anxiety spiraled inside him, but a secret part of him was relieved to have things out in the open.

"Clayton, Kat and I *are* dating."

Kat sucked in a harsh breath and went rigid against his side. She was going to be furious with him.

"What? You're joking." Clayton's brows lowered and his lips pursed into an angry line.

"Dad—" Kat's lips quivered, and Tristan felt her entire body quake.

"We've been seeing each other for a few weeks, since Cambridge. I have only honorable intentions toward her." He almost couldn't believe how strong his voice came out, when everything inside him was flipping on its head. But he meant it; he wanted to date Kat for as long as he could. He didn't want to think about the future when things could change.

The harsh laugh sounded more like a snarl when it escaped Clayton's lips. "Honorable? Tristan, your mother told me all about you. Your womanizing, the affairs, the scandals. I know you're young and reckless, but that doesn't mean you can take my daughter for another notch in your bedpost."

"It isn't like that," Tristan argued, his frustration rolling through him hard enough that he had to clench his fists.

"Dad, you have to let me explain." Kat leaned forward in her seat, but Clayton glowered at her. Her shocked inhalation made Tristan's heart clench.

"I thought you had better sense than that, Katherine. Your studies are crucial. Now is not the time to jeopardize your future by getting distracted by someone like him. He'll drop you and move on to someone else in a matter of days. He has a reputation, Kat. I warned you about him," Clayton growled.

Tristan tried to pull Kat back into the safety of his arms.

"Clayton." Lizzy's voice was soft, wounded. "He's my son..."

Tristan was used to his reputation causing him some discomfort socially, the disapproving looks, the whispers, the articles, but none of that had hurt him like this. Clayton's open anger cut deep.

"If anything, it's my fault, not hers," Tristan said, meeting his mother's eyes. "From the moment I met Kat, I wanted her. Don't blame her for any of this." He turned his gaze back to Clayton, ready for battle.

"At least you have enough sense to accept responsibility. But it's over. Do you understand?" Clayton's imperious declaration was all too familiar.

It was like fighting with his father all over again. He wasn't going to let another man tell him what to do, especially one with no hold over him.

Tristan's lips parted, another protest ready, but Kat spoke up first.

"Dad, you don't get to dictate my life. I'm nineteen. I'm an adult, and my life is all my own. You can accept my choices or not, but you can't control me."

"I can, Katherine. You're still my daughter, and I don't want you getting hurt." The anger that had flared so hot in Clayton's eyes lessened slightly, as though the man was seeing Kat differently for the first time in his life.

"So it's your way or the highway, is that it?" Kat asked.

Tristan sensed she was on the verge of losing her nerve because her hands were trembling when he covered them with his.

"Why don't we wait until we return home to talk about this," Tristan suggested. His heart thudded hard in his chest, and he was strangely nervous. He'd never cared about any woman like this before. Seeing her quarrel with her father because of him and his selfish need to have her...He felt...very *guilty*, because he had no intention of giving Kat up.

"Tristan's right." His mother touched Clayton's shoulder, and while he didn't pull away, he frowned.

"Did you know about this?" Accusation layered his tone, and the look of hurt in Lizzy's eyes shot a bolt of pain through Tristan's chest.

Kat had been right. This would tear their parents apart.

"I—"

"She didn't know." Tristan cut his mother off. "If you have a problem with my relationship with your daughter, you will take it out on me, not Mum. Is that clear?" He met Clayton's eyes with a cold stare. This wouldn't be the first time he'd stood between a cruel bastard and his mother. As soon as he was old enough to argue, he'd put himself between his father and Lizzy time and again, trying his best to protect her.

The fire in Clayton's eyes melted away and his frown faded. "I'm not upset with Lizzy. I'm just upset. I'd never do anything to hurt your mother."

A tender touch brushed Tristan's thigh, and he glanced down to see Kat's hand there. When he looked her way, she was nibbling her lip in concern as she met his eyes. He took her hand and covered it with his own, squeezing gently.

"Let's just talk about this when we get home," Kat said, her gaze darting between him and her father.

The occupants of the car settled into an uncomfortable silence for the rest of their journey. Paul, the driver, kept his gaze decidedly focused on the road ahead, as though he was determined to become invisible.

Tristan's blood pounded like distant war drums against his temples, and he failed miserably at convincing himself that this wouldn't end badly.

When Paul stopped in front of the house, Lizzy and Kat's father got out first. They moved up the icy walkway in a cold silence. When the butler opened the door for them, his pleasant expression faded as he saw their expressions. Tristan gave him a small, forced smile as he was the last to come inside.

"Katherine, I want a word with you *alone*." Clayton gripped her arm firmly, escorting her to the library, where he closed the doors, leaving Tristan and his mother standing in the foyer.

Tristan dropped his head back and stared at the ceiling, trying to breathe.

His mother reached for his hand. "Tristan, how long have you and Kat been...?"

Thrusting his hands into his pockets to avoid his mother's touch, Tristan paced the length of the foyer a few times before he slowed to a stop. The murmur of voices in the library was too soft and muffled by the thick wooden doors.

"We met at Cambridge. Before Christmas break. I've been seeing her on and off." He scraped a hand over his jaw, unable to stop moving, stop pacing, as restlessness rolled through him. He knew it wouldn't go away until Kat was in his arms again.

His mother's lips parted and she exhaled before speaking, her voice low and soft. "On and off?"

He shrugged and finally faced her. "Yes. We had a few fits and starts at first. She didn't like seeing me in the rags with Brianna, and when we found out we were to be stepsiblings, she broke it off then, too. She was afraid of this. She warned me it would break you and Clayton up."

At this, his mother laughed, a quiet, slightly strained sound. "Well, it's not how I imagined our wedding day, or our first Christmas Eve, but it certainly won't break us up."

"I'm not sure if I believe that, Mum. Clayton seems furious." His eyes fixed on the closed library door. *What is he saying to her?* Was he talking her into breaking up with him again? She promised she wouldn't, not as long as they both wanted this. And he still did. More than ever before.

His mother walked in between him and the library door, catching his attention again.

"He couldn't be more different from your father. He talks to me. We don't fight, not like your father and I did. It doesn't mean we don't get upset sometimes, but this won't end our relationship. When two people are in love, they make it work."

"You'd do anything to be with them." Tristan thought of how hard it had been to be without Kat for even a few days. He'd done everything he could to convince her they could make this work.

"Yes, exactly," his mother agreed.

Again, Tristan's focus turned to the library.

"They need time to talk, Tristan. Go make yourself useful and hang stockings above the beds. I haven't done that yet. Then go ask Mrs. George how our pudding fairs this year."

She was deliberately trying to keep him busy and distracted, but Mum was right. He couldn't wear a path into the carpets with his pacing.

With one last glance at the library door, he stalked off to do as his mother suggested. Kat would find him when they were done. He planned to hold her to her promise that she wouldn't walk away. Tristan had to, because he couldn't bear to lose her again.

ABOUT THE AUTHOR

USA TODAY Bestselling Author Lauren Smith is an Oklahoma attorney by day, who pens adventurous and edgy romance stories by the light of her smart phone flashlight app. She knew she was destined to be a romance writer when she attempted to re-write the entire *Titanic* movie just to save Jack from drowning. Connecting with readers by writing emotionally moving, realistic and sexy romances no matter what time period is her passion. She's won multiple awards in several romance subgenres including: New England Reader's Choice Awards, Greater Detroit Book-Seller's Best Awards, and a Semi-Finalist award for the Mary Wollstonecraft Shelley Award.

To connect with Lauren, visit her at:
www.laurensmithbooks.com
lauren@Laurensmithbooks.com

facebook.com/LaurenDianaSmith

twitter.com/LSmithAuthor

instagram.com/LaurenSmithbooks

bookbub.com/authors/lauren-smith